HIGH JOHN THE CONQUEROR

TEXAS TRADITION SERIES
NUMBER TWENTY-FIVE

JAMES WARD LEE, Series Editor

HIGH JOHN
THE CONQUEROR

By JOHN W. WILSON
with an Afterword by
James Ward Lee

FORT WORTH
TEXAS CHRISTIAN UNIVERSITY PRESS
1998

First published by the Macmillan Company, 1948.

Library of Congress Cataloging-in-Publication Data

Wilson, John W. (John Walter), 1920-
High John the conqueror / by John W. Wilson, with an afterword by James Ward Lee.
p. cm.
ISBN 0-87565-186-0 (alk. paper)
I. Title.
PS3545.I6349H5 1998
813'.54—dc21

98-4911
CIP

Cover illustration and design by Barbara Whitehead, Austin, Texas

For FRANCES

INTRODUCTION

In 1984, a good thirty-six years after The Macmillan Company published *High John the Conqueror*, Don Graham of the University of Texas at Austin requested my permission to quote a passage from the novel in a book to be titled *Texas: A Literary Portrait*, on which he was working. Pleased and a little astonished, I agreed. I was pleased that after thirty-six years there was anybody at all who remembered there had ever been such novel, and astonished to learn that it was a work being brought to the attention of students in a famous college course on life and literature of the Southwest. Later, I was equally pleased to find that Graham's book, published in 1985, referred to *High John* as "The breakthrough novel on cotton culture. . . ."

In 1986, I got another pleasant surprise and ego-boost when James Ward Lee, then director of the Center for Texas Studies at North Texas State University, included a review of *High John* in the "Classics of Texas Fiction" series he was doing as a Texas sesquicentennial project and in his book of the same name published in the following year.

High John a classic? That had a nice ring to it, and here I was still alive to hear it! "Is it possible," I was forced to wonder, "is it just barely possible that this book, so long ago put up and hidden away on the back shelves of my mind, still has something to say?"

If so, it says it of life in a time and a place that no longer exist outside the covers of the book; and if this piece of writing, imperfect in craftsmanship as it may be, sensitizes a reader today to even a little of that life and evokes even a small measure of empathy with the people who lived it, then its re-issue takes on meaning and adds a marvel: Read the story and fly back in time to a pre-Civil Rights world during the Great Depression.

You've got to think 1940 (if you're old enough) to realize the frame of reference, In that year Allen Maxwell, editor of the *Southwest Review* at Southern Methodist University, gave the book a beginning impetus toward publication when he accepted and published "Us Goin' to Town," a short story that later was incorporated in the novel. *High John* had pretty well taken shape in my mind by the time that short story was written, but it had to wait out the interruption of World War II for the threads to be picked up, the scenes recollected and the writing completed.

They say you write best about what you know best. I had not consciously set out to write a book about the "cotton culture," but having grown up in it, I certainly knew mule-powered farming and the people who worked at it. Nor had I set out in *High John* to write a sociological novel, but that's the way a good many reviewers saw it when the book was first published.

–Robert Halsband in *The Saturday Review of Literature*: "High John . . . represents the ruthless economic forces that are conquering the farm lands. The Websters, like their counterparts the Joads, are being driven off the land to make way for progress...."

–Paul Crume, in *The Dallas Morning News*: "through a real and human concern for people, Wilson manages to set forth a clearer social message than do most authors "

–Victor P Hass, in *The Chicago Sunday Tribune*: "As a social document, 'High John the Conqueror' builds up surging power."

–And Robert Shaplen also was reminded of the work of John Steinbeck and wrote in the *New York Times Book Review*: "Mr. Wilson seems to have grasped the same sense of slow-moving inevitable force, beyond man himself, that can so easily lift or destroy him"

My goal in writing *High John* was less lofty than to protest against a farming system that meant near-peonage for many or to depict the cotton culture from the black farmer's point of view. Instead, I wrote in a minor but distinct spirit of literary rebellion.

I had a bone to pick with what I was reading in contemporary fiction about farm life and the people who populated the river-bottom plantations. In particular, the folks in the Little Bee Bend Plantation stories of Roark Bradford, which appeared in *The Saturday Evening Post*, did not at all resemble the folks among whom I had grown up and with whom I had worked in the fields. The stories were good, professional, sleek-paper entertainment, but the characters in them seemed to me to be nothing more than black-face comic cut-outs, in no way representing how people on the big farms and the little farms really felt and thought and acted. So a large part of what I had in mind was to write about a black family as individual human beings: as *people*, not as *colored folks*, and certainly not as *darkies*.

This kind of storytelling broke with tradition, but for at least two reviewers when the book issued in late 1948, my success in making the break was clearly limited.

"If you enjoyed the late Roark Bradford and the earlier works of Octavus Roy Cohen," wrote Jack Adams of the *Los Angeles Herald Express*, "run, don't walk, to your nearest bookseller and get High John the Conqueror."

An unidentified reviewer for *Negro Digest* dismissed my attempt to render in writing the sound of local speech: "a Texas author with his heart in the right place but not his typewriter attempts to catch the mood and tempo of Texas sharecropper life. His negro farmers, while colorful and sometimes even warm, wind up as caricatures and dialecticians."

So much for intended rebellion against contemporary characterization of black people in stories written by whites.

* * *

Once or twice in recent years I've been asked if I might want to do some re-writing of *High John* from the vantage point of my present advanced maturity. In effect the question suggests that this could be and maybe should be a lengthier novel and that it would attract a wider readership perhaps if it had more in-depth documentation of farm life and a tad more sex and violence.

But the answer to the re-write question continues to come out "No." This short novel, started before I was age twenty, put aside and overridden by wartime dislocation and resurrected post-war, had best remain the work of a young writer who managed then to catch some sense of the tension underlying a way of life that was rapidly vanishing

So what you have here is the original, unretouched *High*

John the Conqueror, and maybe after all these years it still does have something to say. I am grateful to the Texas Christian University Press for its re-issue.

John W Wilson
Dallas
October 1997

Going east, you pass through a town that is not more than a wide spot in the road, and you never take your foot off the gas. You just ease up a little to make the turn where the highway passes in front of the false-fronted tin post office, and then you straighten out again and pick up speed along a gentle downhill slope of the highway until you see the glass reflectors blinking on the arrow that indicates a sharp right-hand turn. The tires begin to screech faintly when your foot finds the brake, because it has been over a month since you were last through this part of your territory, and you were cruising along without thinking too much about the road and had forgot the sharp turn where the highway makes the approach to the Brazos bridge.

You are a hardware salesman, and the back seat of the car is filled with boxes and order books, but the front seat beside you is vacant except for a half smoked pack of cigarettes, and you just barely have a tinge of lonesomeness, driving through the evening, trying to get to the next town so you can have supper and get up to your room and get some sleep. It is after sundown. Behind you the sky is still red, but in front there is only darkness, except for the tunnel hewn out by your headlights. You meet few cars.

Steel tie rods on the bridge supports clank and rattle, moved by the car's vibration, and you wonder if the damned bridge is going to fall in again. The water is a long way down, and in a quick glance out the window you can see it glinting there below you, reflecting the light from the sky. In the evening the water shows black, glinting because it is shinier than the steep cliffs of the riverbanks; but you think red when you glimpse the river, because that is the only way you know it from having seen it in the daytime.

The bridge behind, the road runs flat across the bottom lands, and your foot comes down on the gas again. You are thinking "Brazos" – the sign on the river bridge is still in your head. The night smell of the water and the weed-grown banks is still in the car, and off to both sides of the road, far back, almost lost in the darkness, you see the dim lights shining where the houses sit. "Christ, what a country!" Cotton growing almost up to the edge of the highway. A wonder they don't have the road plowed up too.

"I'm a bad man, I'm a bad man
From the Brazos land..."

Somewhere you've heard that song, when you got stuck in one of these towns on Saturday. Christ, they're full of niggers then; a white man can't even walk down the sidewalk. Bad man, hell. They all think they're bad when they get a little drunk. Carry a knife and think they could whip Joe Louis. Still, if it were not for these field hands there wouldn't be all this farming along the river, and you wouldn't be doing so well at selling hardware and tractor parts. "But Christ, what a country." Thank God it's Wednesday, and you'll be back in Houston by Saturday, where there's jigaboos, all right, but they don't crowd you off the street.

The highway is the floor of your own private tunnel, a path cut through the evening by your headlights, and the car churns along smooth and quiet, touching sixty on the long, flat stretch. You are alone and you are passing from one town to another, and the road is all there is between, and there is nothing out there but darkness and those little dim flickers of lamplight.

But all you are to the bottoms, brother, all you are to the houses and the people in them is a noise – a quick-mounting, short-lasting roar, and a long, dying swoosh *in the night as you ease her up to sixty-five and pass on, destroying bugs.*

HIGH JOHN
THE CONQUEROR

CHAPTER ONE

Joe Coby's white dog rushed out from under the house to bark at Cleveland. The dog came out snarling and growling; his white hair made him a dim, moving blob in the night. But for his color Cleveland could not have known where the dog was.

"Hey, dog," Cleveland said, growling no less than the animal. "You better get on back. You better not come at me."

The night was dark. The moon had not yet risen, and the sun had been down for over an hour and a half. Stars shone in the clear sky, but their light was barely enough to make the hard surface of the turnrow road that Cleveland walked stand out in contrast to the deeper darkness of the fields that lay to either side.

Cleveland walked with his head down, looking at the road just in front of where his feet would fall. He was himself as dark as the night; his bulk was a part of the shadow that lay across the river bottoms. His feet made little noise. They padded the dirt of the turnrow road and carried him past the front of Joe Coby's house while the dog snuffled alongside him.

The dog ought to have known better than to come barking out at Cleveland like that. He knew Cleveland, had seen him before, smelled his smell. The dog would not have barked except for the fact that it was night, and the road was quiet, and he figured that nobody belonged to be walking the road in front of his yard. He snuffled and held back when Cleveland spoke to him, but then when the man kept walking the dog came on again, a growl deep in his throat, the hair on his neck erect. He came crowding up close to the back of Cleveland's legs.

The yelp that the dog let loose when Cleveland's foot caught him in the ribs just back of the right front leg would have waked Joe Coby and his wife both if they had been at home and asleep. But they were gone down the road someplace, passing the evening before coming home to go to bed, and the house was dark.

"I told you not to come at me," Cleveland said. "I kill me a God-damn' dog do you come at me." He had stopped and turned around to squint his eyes and try to see better in the darkness, to learn whether the kick had settled the dog for the night or whether they were going to have trouble right then. Cleveland's hand was in his pocket, feeling for the long-bladed knife that lay there. "I just as soon kill me a dog," he said aloud.

But Joe Coby's white-haired dog had had enough. He yelped only once, but he kept on whining until he got back under the house, dragging his tail between his legs, turning to look out toward the road. He could see very little; most of what he could see was darkness, because Cleveland was gone; the man had gone on down the road.

Off to the west, the slightly lighter sky where the sun had been last was cut by a fringe of trees that lined the banks of the river. The big Brazos rolled through the July night. The willows on the banks stood tall, but their branches drooped; their long, thin leaves hung motionless. The mosquitoes rose out of the sloughs and backwater ponds and whined above the tall grass and under the branches of the willows. In the clear air above the fields the bullbats flew, beating the air with their wings, sailing, beating the air again to mount higher and higher and then stoop over in a dive, coming down with the wind whistling through their feathers, booming and bellowing as they rounded off just above the tall stalks of dark cotton. A bullbat sailed so close to Cleveland's head that he could feel the air from its passing, but he paid it no mind. He walked on, ambling, his long, thick arms swinging from powerful round shoulders, his feet in heavy muleskin work shoes padding the dirt of the turnrow road.

His own house lay little more than a half-mile beyond Joe Coby's, and as he walked Cleveland was still thinking about the dog, wishing he had been able to land his kick alongside the dog's head and roll him over into the ditch. It gave him pleasure to think about Joe Coby coming home and finding the dog lying there in the ditch.

He was nearly home. His cotton lay to the right of the road, and a few yards farther on the tall fields of corn stood dark and still. Beyond that the house sat with another patch of cotton coming right up to the barn lot and the little square of back yard.

There was no light burning in the house. It was as dark as the fields about it. Cleveland could hear no sound from the house, but when he left the road and crossed the yard, his eyes, grown used to the darkness, made out the form of Ruby Lee sitting in her rocking chair on the front porch.

He stopped before stepping up to the porch, and looked toward her, but Ruby Lee spoke first.

"I didn't know if you'd be home tonight," she said. "You didn't come by the house before you left."

"When did it happen that I got to come tell you every time I go?" Cleveland did not want to talk; he hated finding her there and having to speak to her before he got into the house. He stepped up to the porch floor and strode past her, his shoulders hunched forward even more, his long head seeming to rest on them without any neck for support. His drawn-up attitude made his voice come from deep in his throat.

"Is my supper ready? Did you decide to fix me any supper?"

Ruby Lee got up and followed him into the house. Both of them moved in the darkness with a surety that came from their having complete familiarity with the room—from knowing where the table and the chair stood, where the bed was, and how many steps it was to the door that led into the kitchen. Hardly needing the light, Ruby Lee went to the table to strike a match for the lamp. She answered Cleveland as she moved forward.

"Yo' supper on the stove. It's cold by now, but you didn't say when you was comin' back. I didn't know but what you be gone all night, but I fixed you somethin' to eat. It's on a plate in there."

The match flared, and the lampwick caught. Ruby Lee put the chimney back on and turned the wick up a little. The yellow glow pushed the darkness from the room, but still the light was dim, because the inside of the glass chimney was coated with black soot from the flaring corners of the wick.

Ruby Lee was short. Standing barefoot beside Cleveland she would barely come up to his armpit. But she did not stand close enough to him now for the difference in their heights to be strikingly noticeable. She remained by the table, watching Cleveland, while the lamplight fell full on the right side of her face and left the other side in shadow.

She had been working with her hair. It was combed out straight all around and came down to a line that would just clear the top of her shoulders. It was thick, black, and she had worked dressing into it so that she could manage it when she started pinning it up again.

Her body was rounded, just short of being plump, and her face was round also, with full cheeks and a chin that barely broke the circle contour and kept her from being moonfaced. Touched by the lamplight, her skin shone yellow, but it was in daylight a brown by several shades lighter than Cleveland's. She wore a print dress that had no belt about the waist. The dress hung sacklike from her shoulders and was closed down the front with buttons, but she had left the two top buttons open at her neck because of the warmness of the night, and the cloth was turned back just over the swell of her breasts.

She watched Cleveland go into the kitchen.

"Bring the lamp," he called back. "I can't see to eat in here without no light."

She obeyed him silently, and the lamp seemed brighter in the smaller room as she placed it on the kitchen table. Cleveland got his plate from the stove and dragged a chair from where it stood by the wall. Not until he sat down and hunched himself up to the table did he look up at her. His lips parted a little as he started to speak, but he lacked words for what he wanted to say. He sat there for a moment staring at her, and then fumbled at the front of his shirt, as if unbuttoning it would give him more freedom in speaking.

It didn't. He licked his lips and swallowed, then half turned in the chair to look over his shoulder, avoiding her eyes. "I forgot," he said. "I forgot to get me any water."

Ruby Lee went to the bucket for him. She filled a glass and put it down by his plate, and Cleveland started eating.

"You left yo' hat down at the barn," Ruby Lee said. She pulled up a chair and sat down at the table across from him. "The mules finished they corn and was nickerin' in the lot for water. When I went down there I found yo' hat hangin' on one of the hames."

Cleveland swallowed. He kept working at his plate, mixing his fried egg and bacon and grits. "It ain't the first time I left that hat in the barn. I don't need it except when I'm plowin'—I don't need it except in the heat of the day."

"The chickens mess it up down there," Ruby Lee said. She

was rigidly erect in the straight chair; her hands were folded in her lap as she sat watching Cleveland eat. "I brought it to the house."

Cleveland's fork rattled on the table as his hand banged down. "God damn the hat! You talk to me about the hat! I come home tired, woman—I been in the field all day, and when I try to eat my supper you weary me with talkin' about the hat!" The lamplight caught him full in the face. His broad nose flared out with his breathing while he leaned forward and glared at her across the table.

"You left the field before sundown," Ruby Lee said. "You turned the mules in the lot and went out to the road without comin' through the house. If you so tired with plowin' all day, howcome you go out to walk the road?"

Cleveland sank back in his chair. He quit staring her in the face. Ruby Lee was little, she was quiet most of the time, but she could come at him with a question when he least wanted to answer one.

"Leave off about the road," he said, and his tone was quieter now. Full, his belly's growls answered, he had quit bullying her, and his look was asking her to let him get his thinking straight. "I had to get out and walk a piece. It look like I so restless I couldn't come on in the house and set down." He picked up the glass of water and drank it off, and his head stayed up this time so that he could look across at Ruby Lee.

She was satisfied with what he said. Whether or not his explanation covered the whole matter did not count; he had given in a little, he was not so wound up tight within himself, and instantly Ruby Lee got up to do something for him without being told.

"Let me get you another glass of water," she said. "You want me to fix you another egg?"

Cleveland shook his head. The food helped some. It seemed to soak up some of the weariness from his legs. The water cooled the dry burning at the back of his throat, and he began to wish that he had come on to the house after he finished giving corn to the mules.

He belched. "I got enough," he said. "The supper cold, but it was good. I'm glad you saved it for me."

Ruby Lee put the second glass of water down and remained standing by his chair.

"Since last Sunday," she said, "you been all tied up. Longer than that—you ain't been right since last Sadday night. You didn't used to be mean with me, Clevelan'," she said. "You used to could talk with me. All Monday and all day yestiddy and today it ain't been no livin' with you, and you ain't told me what the trouble was." She touched him. She put her hand on his shoulder and left it there, and he turned in the chair to look up at her.

Cleveland felt the warmth of her body pressing against him. He felt her hand leave his shoulder to rub lightly on his head. He felt himself relaxing as he watched a smile come to her face and saw how the lamp touched her eyes with light and drew shadows across her throat and chest. He felt his heartbeat pick up and begin to cause a feeling of tightness in his chest; he took a deep breath.

He'd been wound up ever since last Saturday; he'd been in the field by sunup every day and home at sundown so tired and sleepy that rest was all he wanted. He had driven himself and worked his mules until they were foam-flecked and leg-weary when he brought them home in the evening, and the next day he drove them again just as fiercely.

His wife's touch was soft. Her close warmth excited him, but still he showed no open response to her, nor did he reach out a hand to touch her.

She moved closer to him. Her hand slipped on across his shoulder. "Let it go," she said. "Let it go tonight. I been waitin' for you to come home. You been in the field all day and I ain't seen you none."

Cleveland leaned away from her. He lifted a hand to remove

hers from his shoulder. "Look," he said wearily, "I can't fool with you tonight. I wish you wouldn't crowd me so."

Ruby Lee stepped back, and her hands dropped to her sides. She stood still as a statue. The cotton dress hung straight down without even a breeze or a breath of air to stir it. Her breast heaved slowly and then she exhaled.

"Clevelan'," she said, "you don't treat me right. You can't blame me for the way you feel. You can't blame me for what I can't help. Clevelan', I wish you'd talk to me."

"I will," Cleveland said, getting up from his chair at the table. He writhed his upper body to stretch the muscles. He straightened his arms, so tense that the tendons showed as hard ridges under his skin. His wristbones cracked as he spread his fingers to ease them and then knotted them into fists. "I'll tell you this—that I'm tired, and I'm goin' in yonder and go to bed. You can put out the light and come on whenever you gets ready to."

He left the kitchen, and Ruby Lee stood where she had moved when he asked her not to crowd him. She heard the bed creak as he sat down on the edge of it. She heard his shoes hit the floor and heard him throw his shirt and pants onto a chair. The bed creaked again as he stretched his body out on it.

Ruby Lee leaned over and blew out the light, then she padded silently on her bare feet through the darkened house. She went out to the front porch again and sat in her rocker.

It was all of thirty minutes later before she heard Cleveland start breathing deep, snoring occasionally. Then she got up and went back into the room and, still in her cotton dress, slipped into the bed as quietly as she could and lay there staring up at the ceiling a long time before she went to sleep.

CHAPTER TWO

Before Cleveland was married, before he and Ruby Lee started in at day labor on John Chaney's big place on the Brazos, there was Cleveland and there was Bully and there was Daly and there was Unca Dempse. "Us goin' to go to town on Sadday!" And there was Tina and there was Vincent and there was Hoodoo and Little Suster. "Us goin' to town on Sadday!"

"The gov'ment check ought to be in the post office when we gets to town," said Bully. "You chop hard from now till then, Little Suster, and I give you twenty cents from the gov'ment check."

"You say next year us ain't goin' to plant so much cotton. What us goin' to do? What I'm goin' to do with them mules if us don't plant no cotton?" Cleveland asked Bully. Cleveland was twenty-four, or close to it, and he was grown big and strong as an ox, and he still lived in the house with Daly and Bully, and Vincent and Hoodoo and Tina and Little Suster.

Unca Dempse was sitting in his rocking chair on the porch near the door. He took his pipe away from his mouth and turned from looking out over the road to stare at Cleveland and Bully. "You goin' to have to work them mules," the old man said. "You goin' to have to work them mules to make them pay for what they eat." He leaned forward to give emphasis to his words, startled by what Cleveland had said about not planting cotton.

"We goin' to plant cotton," Bully told him. "It look like we ought not to plant so much. We got to put in more corn, we got to plant a row of peas between every two rows of corn. Us goin' to use them mules to make us a corn crop and raise us some hogs. Us can't do no good sellin' hogs, but they sho' worth somethin' to put in yo' belly."

Vincent rose up on an elbow where he was lying at the edge

of the porch. "I wish us had them hogs now," he said. "I wish it was time to kill them hogs. I wish I had me some cracklin' corn bread."

"You all the time worryin' about somethin' to eat," Cleveland told his brother. "You talk more about somethin' to eat than all the rest of us put together. Howcome if you talk so much don't you get some meat on yo' bones? You well enough to eat all the time, but when the time come for you to go to the field you sickly. Howcome you all the time makin' Papa holler at you when you supposed to be workin'?"

Vincent was nearly as tall as Cleveland, but he was thin. The overalls he wore bagged on his frame, and his arms stuck out like poles from under his jumper when he had one on. He lay now with the jumper under him, wadded on the porch floor for a pillow while he was stretched out to rest in the cool of the evening. Cleveland and Bully sat with their backs resting against the four-by-four posts that held up the porch roof.

Bully turned on Cleveland. "You leave that boy alone," he warned sharply. "Don't you go pickin' on Vincent any more this e'nin'. You been worryin' at him all day in the field, and one of these times he goin' to rise up from there and hit you with a stick of wood. You leave the rest of them chillun alone," Bully said. "I'll take care of the hollerin' at them if they don't work."

Cleveland mumbled in his throat and glared at Vincent, but quit his complaining and started to roll a cigarette, shaking tobacco into the paper from the sack that he pulled from his breast pocket. His shoes were on the floor beside him and his legs stretched out in front of him. His hands, big-fingered and calloused, were quick with the cigarette as they rolled it, tapered it, and struck a match to light it. Cleveland drew smoke deep into his lungs and exhaled, and the smoke jetted from his nostrils in two streams that were carried away by the quiet breeze blowing from the south.

The sun was down, but the sky was still red in the west, and there was light enough for Hoodoo and Little Suster to play in the yard, heaping the dust in mounds to make graves for their burying ground. In the barn behind the house the chickens squawked and fluttered to their roosts and settled down for the night. Cleveland's cigarette end glowed in the growing darkness while Daly and Tina moved about in the kitchen, putting dishes on the table for supper.

Bully looked toward the southwest, where the light was fading over the treetops and touching the undersides of the floating clouds with pink, but leaving the tumbled masses dark in the evening sky. "Look like it might come on to rain," he said. "That river liable to rise and get muddy again. Corn need a rain, but it wouldn't do that cotton no good. Johnson grass already takin' that cotton below where we was choppin' today. Us got to fight it tomorrow. Clevelan', you got to hitch Old Blue and Pete to the sweepstock and put on a sixteen-inch buzzard wing and double right on back to pullin' middles where us be choppin'. My hoe goin' to be sharp, and I'm goin' to take the lead row and make them chillun step out when we get in the Johnson grass."

"Buzzard wing gettin' might dull," Cleveland said. "We get a point put on it when us go to town Sadday mornin'."

"Us goin' to town Sadday," Hoodoo shouted from the yard. "How long till us get ready to go to town, Papa?" he asked.

"Don't you holler about goin' to town yet," Bully told him. "This just past the middle of the week, and us got work to do before we figure on gettin' in to town."

"Tell them chillun to hush up, and you-all come to supper," Daly called from the kitchen. She came to the door. "Papa, yo' supper ready," she said to Unca Dempse.

The back door was open to let the evening coolness into the house, and from his seat at the head of the table Bully could look out toward the barn lot and still see the outline of the lot fence and the chicken coops and the corncrib. The three mules crunched corn in the shed built against the side of the crib, and in the lot the calf sucked on the bobtailed Jersey cow that Bully had raised from a heifer. Beyond the barn, where the fields began, the land was peaceful with the quiet of a late spring evening, and when the breeze shifted a little it brought to Bully's ears the sound of tree frogs croaking in the trees along the riverbank. There was the moist, growing smell of the river bottoms in the air, and Bully took a deep breath and looked around the table at his family.

"Get out another bucket of milk, Daly," he ordered through a mouthful of bread and meat. "Us got plenty." He swallowed his mouthful and downed a swallow of clabber. "The cow givin' plenty milk, the crop doin' all right, and we gets a gov'ment check Sadday. Times don't be so bad. Le's eat."

The cotton in the bottoms stood three inches high. It had come on fast after being planted in late March, but the grass came on just as fast as the cotton, and Bully had to have all the family in the fields every day trying to whip down the Johnson grass and tie vines before the cotton was choked out. They were chopping for the first time. Bully had planted late because of the high water in the winter that had flooded out over the lowlands until the first of March, and rains throughout the month had kept him from putting a plow in the ground until the sun had a chance to shine for a couple of weeks and dry up the water that stood in the low places. Two shallow sloughs still held the gray, muddy water now, in late May, and when they were chopping near the sloughs Bully had to keep shouting at Hoodoo to get him back from the water's edge where the boy would slip off to try to catch crawfish.

The corn, on the dry, higher ground, was waist-high and doing well. Up to now there had been plenty of moisture for it, and the stalks were green and full with juice. The leaves were dark and full, reaching up toward the light, and Cleveland said they would be eating roasting ears by the middle of June. The corn was clean. They had been through it with hoes and the cultivator, and after they chopped it out and Cleveland dirted back over the roots of the corn, Bully sent Vincent to the field with the Beck mule and the sweepstock with a ten-inch sweep to pull out the middles. He had gone down there in the middle of the afternoon and found the plow lying on its side at the end of a row and the mule trampling down the young corn while she took bites out of the tender leaves growing at the top of each stalk. Vincent was lying down in a middle three rows away, sound asleep with his hat over his eyes.

Bully woke him up with a switch and beat the boy until he hollered, even though he was seventeen years old, and sent him back to the house to whine and sulk all afternoon. Hoodoo took the plow and the mule and finished pulling the middles by sundown, with Bully there to watch him to see that he got every row and managed not to plow up too much corn.

After they finished supper Tina started washing dishes and Hoodoo followed his father toward the front of the house. Daly went in to lie on the bed and rest, but Bully and Cleveland went out to the front porch again. Bully carried a rawhide-bottomed chair with him and placed it leaning against the wall of the house. He cut himself a chew from his plug of Brown's Mule and sat down, looking out to where the road showed light in the evening. He leaned forward in the chair to spit, sending the tobacco juice and loose flakes to splash in the dust beyond the side of the porch, and then he tilted back against the house again. He wiped his mouth carefully with his hand and shifted in the chair, feeling himself relax as some of the tiredness began to flow down through his joints and out of his body. His belly was full, and he had done a day's work and he felt good.

The road in front of the house glowed brighter in the evening as a moon near full began to show above the treetops to the east. The graded surface of the road lay white and quiet, the day's dust settled on it, the wheel tracks and the bird tracks pressed into the dirt, with the eastern sides of the depressions etched in tiny shadows by the slanting light of the rising moon, the white rocks of the roadbed gleaming, each broken side reflecting the light, making the road shine, making it white where it curved up out of the deep woods farther back in the bottoms and ran through the clear space in front of Bully's house before bending and dipping once more to cross Spring Creek and wind again toward town.

CHAPTER THREE

"I didn't get to tell you last night," Ruby Lee said. "I didn't get no chance to tell you, but Mr. John come by here yestiddy."

"He come by here nearly every day," Cleveland grunted. "What he want this time?" The lamp still burned on the kitchen table, but the increasing morning light was causing the yellow flame to appear feeble. The sun would be up in a little while. The clouds in the east were touched with pink, and outside in the fields the cotton nodded and the corn leaves rustled in the damp breeze that always came up just before dawn and blew until about nine o'clock in the morning.

Cleveland was finishing his breakfast, and Ruby Lee was over by the stove where she had a dishpan of water on to warm for washing the dishes. Cleveland had his back to her and was busy cleaning his plate. He was only half dressed. The shoes on his feet were not yet laced, a fresh jumper hung on the back of the chair, and his broad back seemed to bulge out above the waist of his overalls. The overall straps crossed in the middle of his back, and the high bib in front did little to cover the brown expanse of his chest. Sparse, short hairs curled over the edge of the denim cloth. Cleveland was heavy; it took a big breakfast to keep him going until dinnertime, and Ruby Lee had put a heaped plate of bacon and eggs before him.

He had complained about having to eat light bread for breakfast—it did not go too well with syrup and bacon grease

—but Ruby Lee had got up a little too late to fix hot bread before it was time for him to go to the field. After she did get to sleep she felt so worn-out that she lay there like a log, and Cleveland had to shake her to get her awake so she could be working on the breakfast while he went out to feed and water the mules and get the harness on them.

No matter if Cleveland did come home mad in the evening, no matter if he did go to bed angry at night—he still wanted his food. He had to have it if he was going to make a day in the field.

"I aimed to tell you," Ruby Lee said. "He come by here to ask could I go in to town."

Cleveland turned around in his chair. "When? What for? When he want you to go to town?"

"He just asked," Ruby Lee said. "He say they lookin' for somebody to come up there and help with the house." She carried the dishpan over to the side table.

"They live in town," Cleveland said. "Ain't they got somebody there all the time? Can't they get no help in town?"

"I don't know," Ruby Lee answered. "All I know is what he ask when he stopped by here yestiddy."

"Why the man talk like that?" Cleveland demanded. "Why he come by here and talk to you like that? He know it take both of us if we goin' to keep this crop clean." Cleveland thought he had heard the truck stop yesterday, but he had been down behind the corn, finishing off the last of the older cotton, and he could not tell for sure. John Chaney ran that pickup all day long anyhow. He was always stopping somewhere along the turnrow to see how the work in the fields was coming, and Cleveland could not know for sure just where the truck had stopped.

"That must have been after I seen him and talked with him," Cleveland said. "Howcome he didn't say somethin' to me about it then?"

"I don't know," Ruby Lee said. "It was yestiddy after dinner. He stayed in the truck and I went out in the yard to talk to him."

"What did you say?" Cleveland got up from the table and carried his plate over to put it down by the dishpan. "What did you tell him when he ask you?"

"What could I tell him?" Ruby Lee said shortly. "I say I don't know. I say it look like we got all we can do here."

"We got that cotton to get clean," Cleveland said. "If us goin' to fool with makin' a crop out here we got to work on it. It take you and me both; I can't chop out that cotton and plow it at the same time, and we goin' to get caught by the rain if we don't get it laid by."

Cleveland picked up his jumper. He slipped the overall straps over his shoulders and let the bib drop to his waist while he slipped into the jumper. "I quit before we fool around with this crop any longer. I leave out from here before I piddle with it all the time and lose a year's work."

"You don't need to holler at me," Ruby Lee said, plunging the plates into the soapy water. "I didn't tell the man I would go. I know what we got to do. I put him off as best I could."

"I wish you put him off so he wouldn't come back," Cleveland grunted as he finished lacing his shoes and straightened up to step toward the back door. "He all the time down here foolin' around. He all the time down here to look at this crop. If he don't like the way I farm why don't he tell me so? I don't want to work for no man that fault me all the time."

Ruby Lee turned around to look at Cleveland. Her hands stayed in the dishwater.

"He ain't fault you," she said. "He just come down here to see how you makin' out. This the first crop, Clevelan'. Let's make it out. Let's get along with the white man so we keep the place and stay here. I don't want to fool with no day labor any more; we done had enough of that. I rather we had our own place and work for ourselves."

"So had I," Cleveland told her. "But this place ain't ours.

We might think we workin' for ourselves, but we ain't. If we workin' for ourselves howcome the man worry so much about comin' down here all the time?"

"We been talk and holler about all this before," Ruby Lee said wearily. "Don't get mad now, it's too early in the mornin'." She wiped her hands on the dish towel and turned around to lean her hips against the table. "We wanted to get the place," she said. "We kept hopin' to get the place, and we got it now, so let's make out with it till we get one crop anyhow."

"Then you tell the man," Cleveland said from the door. "You tell him to get somebody else. You tell him you can't go. That young cotton goin' to need walkin' through behind me, and I want you to bring yo' hoe to the field and chop this mornin'." He finished buttoning his jumper and looked around for his hat.

"This my day to go to the sto'," Ruby Lee said, walking out to the middle of the room. "I ain't been since last week. We done used up everything we brought from town Sadday, and if you want me to have anything to fix for yo' dinner I got to go to the sto' this mornin'."

"That young cotton goin' to get in the grass," Cleveland said. "It need walkin' through with a hoe if we goin' to keep it out the grass."

He stepped down out of the kitchen door and was gone across the yard toward the barn before Ruby Lee had time to say anything more to him. The harness rattled on the mules in the lot as he looped the traces over the hames and gathered the rope lines up short. He jumped up to sit sideways on the Pete mule's back and was gone out through the lot gap to the turnrow road while Ruby Lee stood in the kitchen door and watched him.

In the east it was broad daylight. The red edge of the sun was just beginning to show above the distant rim of trees that edged the broad, flat fields of the river bottom, and all up and down the road the teams were moving to the field. Up toward the headquarters buildings there was the sound of tractor motors, and the big trucks coming out from town with loads of day hands for chopping turned off the paved highway and came down the dirt roads that ran through the cotton, lifting heavy clouds of the dry, red dust to be caught up and spread by the early morning breeze.

The day was clear except for a few small clouds that floated in the east, and somewhere down the turnrow toward Cul Sally's place there was somebody singing; but when Ruby Lee turned back into the kitchen to finish her work she was silent. She moved slowly and wearily, but not from lack of sleep. Ruby Lee didn't feel like singing this morning. She wiped her hands again on her skirt as she went toward the table and, bending forward until the heat from the chimney was on her face, she blew out the light.

CHAPTER FOUR

Dull black and rich with sediment left by years of standing floodwater, the earth gleamed under the sun, and cotton roots searched downward to suck up moisture from below the surface where heat hardened the small clods and baked them into rough grayness.

With Daly and Bully and Vincent and Tina and Hoodoo and Little Suster chopping, six rows at a time, the family walked through the field and left it clean, and the trees beyond the turnrow along the riverbank came closer with every round they made.

"Us goin' to finish this field by five o'clock," Bully said. "Us goin' to get done this e'nin'."

"Us want to get started to town early in the mornin'," Daly said. "If them clouds keep on comin' and pilin' up it goin' to rain before long, and I wants to get on into town and get started back home before us gets wet."

"That rain goin' to hold off," Bully told her. "I hope it do, because this cotton don't need no more rain right now. If this bottom get wet again us can't get back in here to chop for a month, and by that time the grass be done taken it. I just as soon it don't rain no more till July."

Cleveland stopped his team and walked to where the rest of the family was stopped at the end of a row. "Us got to grease that waggin before we hitch up to go to town," he said. "I been aimin' to grease that waggin for a week, but us been so busy down here in the bottoms that I ain't had time."

"We grease it in the mornin'," Bully said. "Us goin' to get up early and grease that waggin and we ride on into town like it wasn't nothin' botherin' us. The check goin' to be there and I'm goin' to pay you chillun yo' choppin' money tomorrow. If it wasn't for the gov'ment check I don't know how we would make out this year."

All of them were up by sunup Saturday morning. Cleveland ran the wagon out of the shed and greased it before hitching up the blue mule and the Pete mule. Vincent put a sack of corn nubbins in the wagon for the noontime feeding of the mules, and Bully came out of the house with two chairs and a quilt to make soft seats for Daly and Tina.

They all ate a bite of breakfast, but the children were too excited to want much. "Us goin' to town," Hoodoo and Little Suster said.

At six o'clock they left, with Bully driving and Daly and Tina in the two chairs. Unca Dempse sat at the front of the wagon with Bully. Little Suster sat on the sack of corn nubbins, and Vincent and Cleveland hung their legs over the side of the wagon. Hoodoo ran along behind for a while, then got on the coupling pole and rode.

They made the trip to town in good time, though the mules had walked slowly in the beginning. Crossing Spring Creek, their hoofs had rung hollowly on the bridge, and during the long pull out of the bottoms the family had ridden quietly, with only Bully speaking to the mules occasionally, or clicking his tongue at them as they strained up the winding hill road before they turned on to the main road to town.

The sun was bright and hot, climbing above the trees and the housetops. The long morning shadows were cool, but the air was still and the day would be warm. Heat already was beginning to rise from the black-topped streets when the wagon entered the city limits. Last evening's thunderhead, that had hung in the southwest, was gone, but low-drifting tufts of cloud floated in the morning sky.

"We goin' to have to leave early," Daly said. "It goin' to rain again, and I wants us to get on home before we get wet. I don't want to be gettin' back there tonight wet through to the skin and weary with ridin' in the rain."

Unca Dempse spoke for the first time since he had climbed into the wagon. "The sun shinin', Daly," he said. "The rain done through. Why don't you just let it dry off and be hot for a while?"

The mules, unmindful of the cars that passed them on the street, made their way through the traffic, and Bully turned through an alley into the vacant lot that lay behind a grocery store. Only two wagons were ahead of him, and he drove to the side of the lot where the store building cast its shadow and pulled up there.

"We here," he said. "Clevelan', help me get these mules unhooked."

Five minutes later Bully was in the post office lobby while the rest of the family waited for him on the steps outside.

The window was not yet open. Bully looked at the drawn shades and waited. He was not alone; twelve men waited with him in the lobby, leaning against the glass-topped table, propped against the wall, or staring at the bulletin board with its reward offerings and its notification of civil service examinations. Book Turner was there, and Laro Tinsley, and Joe Coby from out in the Brazos bottoms.

"They goin' to open today?" Bully asked. Worry was in his

voice and his eyelids blinked while he fingered the buttons at the bib of his overalls. "They don't stay closed all day on Sadday, do they?"

"Wait to the clock strike," Book Turner said. "The window open when the clock strike eight. They don't open up till eight o'clock."

"I hadn't been in here in a long time," Bully said apologetically. He might be from the country, but Book Turner didn't live in town either, and Bully figured that it was just pure chance that Book knew these things. "Us don't get no letters except from the gov'ment, and I hopes they send me one today. You looking for a check too?"

"I been lookin' for my check," Book Turner said. "I come here at it last week and they told me there wasn't no check. I made a trip in to town in the middle of the week with a load of hay, and they still wasn't no check. It bound to be here today. I'm got to get that check," Book said. "I'm got to pay some on my bill at the sto' before they let me have any more feed, and them mules got to have they oats if they goin' to make a crop for me this summer."

The frown came back to Bully's face. His eyes widened slightly and he turned to look again at the closed window. "They supposed to be here today. I heard it in town last week that them checks supposed to be here today."

Both Bully and Book Turner leaned against a table that stood next to the swinging door which opened into the post office lobby from the street. Bully was shorter than Book, and he had to look up a little to see the bigger man's face while they were talking. They were dressed almost identically in muleskin work shoes, clean overalls, and blue chambray shirts. The tag of a pack of Bull Durham tobacco dangled from the breast pocket of Book's shirt, just clearing the top of the overall bib, and Bully's back pocket bulged with a paper-wrapped plug of tobacco. Bully's hat was felt, and Book Turner wore a pinch-crowned, battered straw. That was the only difference.

Both of them shuffled their feet and straightened to move out of the way when a white man came through the swinging door and went to his box for mail. Hard-heeled cowboy boots thudded across the granite floor as the white man gathered his letters and papers and turned to the table to straighten them.

"Mornin', Mr. John." Bully dipped his head as he spoke.

John Chaney looked up from his papers, his eyes roving past the still faces of the waiting Negroes until they found Bully.

"How you, Bully?" he said then, and his greeting was shrill and high, but loud also, seeming to fill the small, crowded lobby. Bully wished he had not spoken to the white man, because now the eyes of all the others were turned on the two of them. While Bully and Book Turner talked, the conversation around them continued—man talked to man, neighbor to neighbor; but when Bully and the white man spoke to each other the talk died and the laughter dropped off and the gestures ceased and all the other overall-clad, blue-shirted figures shifted eyes to watch and stood still to listen.

Bully would have done the same if another man had spoken to John Chaney first, but now that he was the one who had opened his mouth he felt uncomfortable and wished that he had avoided the white man and had kept from speaking to him, although they were neighbors, with their places joining on the river.

The words that passed between them were not much in the way of talk. John Chaney had pushed his straw hat back and was mopping at his face already, in spite of the coolness of the morning. "You in town early, Bully," he said. "You in here to get your check?" He gathered up his mail as he spoke; he was in a hurry to go.

"Yassuh, Mr. John," Bully said. "I hope it be there." Behind him he heard the noise of the window opening and the shuffle of feet as Book Turner and the others lined up to ask for their mail. But Bully did not move. He could not turn his back on the white man.

Chaney said nothing more, but pulled his hat back over his forehead and turned to go out the door, and by that time Bully was left to be the last in line.

"The window open now," Hoodoo announced from the door. He had climbed the steps to look in through the glass. "He waitin' to get up there—they people ahead of him."

"Come away, Hoodoo. Get away from that door." Daly started toward him. "You blockin' people's way. Somebody push that door open and hit you right in the face."

Hoodoo came down the steps to rejoin the family in the shade to one side on the broad landing of the post office steps. Unca Dempse sat on the marble banister, Daly stood holding Little Suster by the hand, and Cleveland was making a cigarette while he leaned against the wall of the building. Vincent sat on the steps with his back toward the rest of them, looking out into the street; and Tina was to one side where she could look up at the town clock which crowned the city hall on the other side of the square.

All of them saw John Chaney enter the post office. When he came out again their heads turned while their eyes followed him as he went down the steps and crossed the street to his parked truck.

The white man was busy with his papers when he left the building, and did not notice them, and none of them spoke any greeting. None of them said anything, except Unca Dempse, whose eyes were a little weak. "Wasn't that Mr. John?" he asked, watching the truck move down the street. "Daly, wasn't that Mr. John Chaney?"

"Unh-hunh," Daly said, and that was when Hoodoo made his announcement from the door.

"I hope he get the check," Cleveland said, jetting smoke from his cigarette to blow out the match he had used to light it. "I won't have a bit of money if he don't get the check today."

Vincent laughed. "Neither will nobody else." He turned his thin body around as he stood up, and jammed his hands deep in his overalls pockets. "Neither will nobody else but me, and I got a dollar I saved from last time Papa paid me off." He pulled his right hand out and opened it to show two fifty-cent pieces shining in his palm. His eyes were bright and the whine was gone from his voice, but there was a weakness in it, a sly whisperiness that was the product of either craft or sickness. He joyed to have, for the moment, a sense of domination over Cleveland. The two fifty-cent pieces made him something more than the rest of them, and the circumstances had turned just right to give him a chance to show it off.

His hand snapped shut and darted back into his pocket as Cleveland started forward from the wall.

"What you doin' with money?" Cleveland demanded. "Where you get that dollar?"

"Get on from here. Don't you come at me, Cleveland," Vincent said, ducking his head and backing away. He was nearly as tall as his brother, but the difference in the breadth of their bodies was made even more apparent by Vincent's height. He was thin as a snake, and his skin was dry and crusty. His face was wizened, and his eyes, sunk deep in their sockets, narrowed to slits as he drew his head down between his shoulders like a turtle going back into his shell and raised one elbow as if to ward off a striking fist.

Cleveland spoke with disgust. "I ain't comin' at you. All I ask is where did you get that dollar? You never told nobody you had that money."

"I been had this dollar," Vincent said, relaxing as he saw that Cleveland was not going to try to take it away from him, and feeling his importance grow again. "I didn't spend but a dime in town last Sadday and I saved this dollar from then. I didn't go throwin' my money around. I didn't spend nothin' on no Ruby Lee. I didn't—" He jumped as Cleveland grabbed at him, and twisted to get away from his older brother.

"Cleveland!" Daly spoke sharply. "Leave him be—he just makin' fun." But she whirled on Vincent. "You mind how you talk about what other people do with they money, else I let Cleveland go on and get hold of you."

"Never mind about what I do." Cleveland glowered at Vincent but moved back again to lean against the post office wall. "When I want you to tell me how to spend my money, I ask you."

Tina moved over to stand closer to her mother, so that she would be in a safe zone if what she said made Vincent angry. "You got sick last Sadday," she said triumphantly. "You went back to the waggin with Unca Dempse. That's howcome you didn't spend all yo' money in town."

The thing had not come off. His attempt at domination failed to work, and Vincent was reduced to mumbling again. The coins clinked in his pocket. He moved off to sit down on the banister by Unca Dempse. "I wish," he whined, "I wish you-all wouldn't all the time pick at me."

Hoodoo and Little Suster, both a little lost in what was going on, had stood wide-eyed; but now, this excitement gone, Hoodoo's energy bubbled up again and drove him to the door, where he put up a hand to shield his eyes so he could look in when he pressed his face close to the glass. He straightened and backed down the steps, his bare feet somehow keeping him from falling.

"Here come Papa," he shouted. "Here he come now. He done been to the window and got it."

Bully was grinning as he came out the door.

"You got the check?" Daly asked. Her face was unsmiling, anxious. Fine lines wrinkled her forehead, and her dark eyes repeated the question as she looked up at him. The faces of the others held an almost identical look. All turned their eyes toward the door and the top of the steps, tilting their heads back a little so they could watch Bully as he came toward them. Even Unca Dempse got up from his seat and moved forward to hear what Bully had to say.

"What this in my hand?" Bully asked, laughing. "There

the envelope with my name on it; I reckon the check inside."

"What's that, Papa?" Hoodoo wanted to know. "What's that you got in yo' other hand?"

"Us got two letters," Bully said. "Us got two letters from the gov'ment, and us goin' to be rich today. Unca Dempse, this one here for you. It look like yo' pension check done got here."

CHAPTER FIVE

Cleveland's team went sidling off across the cotton that grew next to the turnrow, trampling the plants, dragging the rope lines over the rows, until Cul Sally went after the mules and got hold of a line. Joe Coby had caught Buddy Boy Taylor's team and was leading it back down the road, and already there was a crowd of choppers gathered on the turnrow where Cleveland and Buddy Boy stood facing each other.

Other choppers, their hoes over their shoulders, saw the group and started walking faster. Two hands riding cultivator teams whipped the mules to a trot when they saw Cleveland and Buddy Boy standing there.

The two men shuffled their feet in the dirt. They were still talking; nobody had been hit yet.

Cleveland had his head drawn down between his shoulders, his back bowed, his long arms dangling.

Buddy Boy was a shade slighter in build, but he was taller than Cleveland. His skin was lighter also, his nose thinner; but he had muscles under his shirt. He had strength in his arms, and his round head appeared to be hard as a rock. The hair was clipped short, leaving the dark, tight skin to show the shape of his skull. He had knocked his hat off his head when he slid down from his team and came up to face Cleveland.

"I just ask you what yo' wife think," Buddy Boy Taylor was saying. "I just ask you what yo' wife think about you slippin' out to other women."

"Why is it yo' business that you worry about what I do?" Cleveland answered him. "You a lie. You a damn lie, and you know it."

"I seen you last night," Buddy Boy said. He still kept from closing in on Cleveland. He still avoided getting too close to him. "I seen who it was leave Lometa's house before I got there. I tell you she my woman, Clevelan'. You better stay home with yo' wife."

"You watch how you talk, Buddy Boy. I come to the field to do my work. When my work done I walk the road to where I please."

"I tell you now to stay away. I tell you now that you mess with Lometa and you goin' to have to mess with me."

Cleveland had enough. He had been all right until Buddy Boy stopped him. "I told you to watch out, Buddy Boy," he said. "I ain't fool with yo' whore."

He was waiting for Buddy Boy's fist and he caught it on his arm. He pushed in, his feet shuffled him forward, and his hand went out to get Buddy Boy by the throat of his shirt.

Buddy Boy pumped his arms, and his fists thudded into Cleveland's ribs, but Cleveland came on. His left hand twisted tighter in Buddy Boy's shirt front; his right hand dived into his pocket and grasped the long-bladed knife.

"You come at me," he said. "I'm goin' kill me a God-damn' nigger."

The others saw him pulling the knife. Joe Coby shouted, and Cul Sally called from the road where he stood trying to quiet Cleveland's team, hold his own mules, and see what was going on at the same time. "Hold them fools," Cul Sally called. "Knock them fools apart. Here come Mr. John—here come the truck!"

John Chaney's pickup truck was coming down the turnrow road. The sun was beginning to show over the trees to the east, and the white man wanted to be out in the bottoms to see that his hands got to the field early. Cul Sally could have seen the dust kicked up by the truck sooner had he not had his hands full with the mules and had he not been trying to see over the heads of the choppers who stood between him and the two circling men.

But it was too late, and the white man was on them before they could get Buddy Boy and Cleveland pulled apart. John Chaney put on the brakes so hard that the wheels of his truck slid in the dust and sent it boiling up around the group that stood at the edge of the field.

The white man was out of the cab as soon as the truck stopped. The choppers found business on down the road. They backed away; they went on toward their field as fast as they could without running, but kept turning to look back over their shoulders.

John Chaney was tall, taller than either Cleveland or Buddy Boy, and he was thicker through the waist. His long legs carried him across the road with a couple of steps, and he was between the two men, shoving them apart. He had a high voice, a thin voice for a big man, but it had volume when he was angry. And it had volume now.

"What the hell?" he asked. "What the hell are you black sons of bitches tryin' to do? Why ain't them teams hooked up? Why ain't you-all in the field?"

John Chaney never did believe in bluffing. There was no bluffing now—he just walked in and shoved and shouted out to put the fear of God into the two men. To get them stopped in a hurry he had to make them more scared of him than they were mad with each other, and he could have done that merely by pulling up beside them in the truck. Both Cleveland and Buddy Boy, when they felt his hands on them, sobered quickly and moved back without resisting.

Cleveland's knife hand was on the off side, and he slid the knife back into his pocket before the white man could see it.

"I don't care what the trouble is," John Chaney said. "But there's goin' to be more if you don't get them teams in the field. Buddy Boy, I didn't take you off from driving truck to fight on the turnrows. You better get them mules hooked up."

He turned to Cleveland. "You wait," he said. "You let Cul Sally go on and hitch up that team and you wait here for what I've got to say."

John Chaney stood in the middle of the road until the men and the teams had moved away toward the field where the cultivators stood. His boot heels left little prints in the dust, and his tall figure loomed up large in the morning sunlight, which threw his long shadow out across the dew-wet cotton on the west side of the road.

He pulled a big white handkerchief from his hip pocket and wiped at his face and neck with it before turning again to move toward Cleveland.

The white man looked at Cleveland for a minute, and Cleveland responded by standing in the road like a tree that might have grown there and died and been burned out to a solid, black stump of hard wood which was rooted but had no life. Cleveland stood and waited for John Chaney to speak, and if his mind were as blank as was his face, then there should have been an audible click when his thinking stopped.

With John Chaney there, Cleveland had no time to think longer about Buddy Boy. He was getting his breathing under control, and though his anger still burned in him, it was dying down from active rage to a sullenness that kept his jaw tight clenched, his eyes half closed, and his lips protruding.

"I don't know what the trouble is this morning," John Chaney said. "And I don't care. But I know this, Cleveland—I know that you been goin' around here all swelled up for nearly a month, and all anybody's got to do is say one word to you and you pick a fight with him."

"I ain't pick this fight," Cleveland mumbled. "I ain't start this."

"And, by God, you won't finish it," John Chaney said. "This crop's too far behind for you God-damn' people to be cuttin' each other up and making me short of hands." The white man's voice was back to normal now. Familiar as it was to him, the odd, high sound of Chaney's speech would have struck Cleveland as funny had it not been for the fact that there was nothing funny about the way he had to stand there and listen to what was being said. "How long you been out here, Cleveland?" John Chaney asked. "How long have I had you on this place?"

Cleveland tried to remember. He had to get Buddy Boy entirely out of his mind, and he had to forget about his anger so he could make an answer to the white man.

"This my first crop, Mr. John," he said. "I been here nearly a year, but I worked day labor for you last summer."

John Channey nodded. In his mind he went back to the summer before, to place Cleveland among the new hands he had hired and brought out to the bottoms to work the big fields and get his crop made. "If you hadn't been good, Cleveland," he said, "you wouldn't be on that place you got now. I let you and your wife have that place and move into that house because I figured you could make a crop for me. But I tell you, Cleveland, if you can't get along with these other people out here I'm goin' to have to move somebody in there that can."

"I get along," Cleveland said defensively. "Buddy Boy and me just tusslin'."

"You're lying, Cleveland. You know you're not telling me the truth. In another minute you'd have cut that boy." John Chaney shook his head. "I've seen how you are. I don't believe you're mean, but, by God, you can blow up in a hurry. You got to watch out, Cleveland—I don't want to have any trouble out here in these bottoms while this crop is in the mess it's in now."

Cleveland said nothing. He stood there waiting for the white man to finish with him. He listened, but it was no matter what the man said. The fight was not of Cleveland's making. He was no longer mad with Buddy Boy; his anger was over and done with as quickly as it had flared up.

Cleveland ought to have laughed at Buddy Boy for thinking he had fooled around with Lometa. He would have laughed except that there was too much truth in it. He had thought he could fool around with her; it had been done before. Buddy Boy knew that any man in the bottoms could fool with that woman. That was why he was so mad. But Buddy Boy had no call to worry; Lometa would have nothing to do with Cleveland.

He had walked that far down the road by the time it began to get dark, but all he got at Lometa's house was a drink of water. "Where Ruby Lee?" Lometa said. "Why don't you bring yo' wife to see me?" She laughed at him; he couldn't touch her. All she'd let him do was give her a cigarette.

"Hunh-unh, Clevelan'," Lometa said. "You go on home. You didn't come down here because you want to see me. I ain't got no bed for you to sleep on when yo' wife won't let you in the house."

He'd have hit her and knocked her teeth down her throat if she had not kept on laughing at him. She knew how to handle Cleveland. She made him feel like a barebutted little boy, and all he could do was leave. That made it a little hard on Joe Coby's dog.

Cleveland blinked and started listening to the white man again. John Chaney was done with him for this morning. "That's all I got to say, Cleveland. Go on down there to your cultivator. I just wanted to tell you to watch out." The words were chopped out short, and his nod was one of dismissal. He stepped into the truck and drove off toward the headquarters buildings grouped a mile away.

Cleveland's cultivator stood not more than a hundred yards distant, and Cul Sally already had the team hitched up and was standing there waiting for Cleveland to take the reins and the plow handles.

"What Mr. John say to you?" Cul Sally wanted to know. "Did he cuss you for fightin' in the field?" Cul's eyes were eager, his body slightly tense, as he shuffled his feet in the dirt, not certain of the way Cleveland would be feeling.

Cul was short and barrel-round. His skin was darker than Cleveland's. He was black, a deep, rich color which was made even richer by the gleaming perspiration which popped out on his forehead and his neck and helped the brightening sun put highlights in his skin. He was a year older than Cleveland, but he was a little cautious with the bigger man. Cleveland was too changeable to joke with, too quick to anger to question when the questions touched close to a sore spot.

"What did he say about you and Buddy Boy?" Cul Sally asked.

"Nothin'." Cleveland took the rope lines out of Cul Sally's hands. The ends of the lines already were knotted together, and he slipped the rope over his neck. He took hold of the cultivator handles. "He didn't say nothin' about the fight. He just say this crop in the grass and he want to see it clean."

Cleveland reached up with his right hand and caught hold of the rope line. He swung it to smack the side of the Pete mule; he spoke to the team, and the mules started forward. The cultivator sweeps straddled the cotton row and turned up the red, fresh dirt. The small growth of Bermuda, of crab grass, the beginning shoots of maypops and tie vines were turned over by the sweeps or covered by the moist dirt. The cotton on the west side of the road, in the last field on the place that Cleveland was cropping on third-and-fourths for the white man, nodded in the breeze that was beginning to spring up and blow from across the river.

Cul Sally stood on the turnrow for a minute longer, looking after Cleveland. He saw the team, the blue mule and the Pete mule, walking toward the far end of the first row in the field;

he watched how the mules stepped out, fresh in the morning, with their ears held up, their tails switching at flies whether or not there were any. He watched how Cleveland followed the plow, head down, eyes on the cotton, intent. The way Cleveland could put everything else out of his mind when he was in the field had been a source of continued wonder for Cul as long as he had known the younger man. Cul was a good farmer but he hated to go to the field, and if he sang while he was there it was not because his work gave him pleasure. He sang to keep his mind off his work. But Cleveland took a joy in working with a crop that Cul could never understand. Cleveland loved it as some people love good whisky. His thoughts, his muscles, the movements of his body, all were joined in an intense concentration of effort that showed how completely he was absorbed in the single operation of plowing. The way it looked to Cul Sally, Cleveland might not ever have heard of John Chaney, nor of Buddy Boy Taylor, for all the difference it seemed to make to him now.

CHAPTER SIX

Now, you take the town on Saturday. Take it on Saturday and look at it, and compare it with the town on any other day of the week. You might begin to figure that you have two different towns—one for the white man, one for the Negro. On Saturday there's that "Lord God Almighty have mercy on my wearied soul" feeling that a clerk has when he opens the door to a dry goods store or sweeps up between the stands in a grocery store. He knows he is going to be there until midnight, standing on his feet, straightening merchandise until the world looks level. He knows that on Saturday he is going to work, that he won't have time to slip out for a cup of coffee in the middle of the afternoon, and he wishes Saturday were one day in the week that didn't happen.

All week long there has been the white man's town, with nearly empty streets and the slow move of everyday trade. The salesmen have called at the grocery stores and the hardware stores, taken their orders, and left. The sheriff has been sitting in his chair in front of the hotel every day from nine o'clock in the morning until ten o'clock at night, except for Wednesday when he rode out to the edge of the city limits to the cattle auction and bought a couple of steer yearlings. The bank has opened up at nine o'clock and closed at three in the afternoon, and the tellers, the clerks, and the bookkeepers have had it easy. Nothing more to take care of than the regular store deposits, not many out-of-town checks to write up, few note payments to enter. But Friday a shipment of money from the Federal Reserve in Houston comes in on the noon train—silver dollars, plenty of silver dollars, because in chopping time the pay roll is big. Every man who has a place out there along the big Brazos is going to be paying off his hands in those big, round, solid American dollars; and after the paying off you would begin to think you no longer have the white man's town. It is Saturday.

There is money in the hand and money in the pocket. Cash money for spending, and the doors to the stores stand open. The sun rises higher in the sky, the morning grows toward noon, and the streets crawl with people come to town on Saturday. The cool shadows thrown by the store fronts and awnings on the east side of the street draw the standers and the talkers, but the walkers and lookers move regardless of the sun. What does it matter how the sun shines in town when all week long it has burned down in the middle of a wide field? Who complains about a little sun when there's money in the pocket and the doors to the stores stand open? Let the old, the weary, the lame, and the feeble gather on the shady side of the street to knit in groups for talking and for spraying the sidewalk with bright brown tobacco juice. The walkers and the lookers will move, forgetting the sun, and crowd the stores, and buy, and drink ice water from the water keg standing by the door; and that clerk is there on his feet, making sales, wishing for his cup of coffee and knowing damn well he won't get it until closing time, and closing time is midnight. You might begin to think the white man's town is gone, but you'd be wrong. The people have come in from the bottoms along the big Brazos, and from the farms up on the Navasot'; they crowd the streets and talk. But with a deputy driving, a second deputy in the back seat, the sheriff prowls the main drag in his car. He prowls the back alleys and the streets of Freedmantown. It is still the white man's town.

"Come with me, Tina. Come with me, Little Suster," Daly said. "Come with me and let's buy us groceries now and put them in a box and leave them in the sto'. Let's get that done and then we have time to walk about."

She took Little Suster by the hand and started down the street, threading her way through the crowd, with Tina trying hard to stay by her mother's side, for Daly walked fast when she had a purpose. She was big enough to make her way, intent enough not to stop and talk to the women who called greetings to her, and Little Suster, gripping hard on Daly's hand, had nearly to run as they sailed off toward the store.

"Let them be gone to the sto'," said Cleveland. "I got business to tend to on Railroad Street. Gi' me my money, Papa, and let me get started." He held out his palm for Bully to count five dollars into it. "You comin' with me, Vincent, or you goin' to knock about by yo'self?"

"You go on," Vincent said. "I wouldn't be with you long anyhow. What you do and what I do ain't the same."

Cleveland glowered at his brother but made no answer. He turned away to walk up the street, cross the railroad, and be lost in the moving crowd.

That left Vincent and Bully and Hoodoo standing in front of the bank.

"Here yo' dollar, Vincent," Bully said. "And Hoodoo, here yo' fifty cents. You-all be careful how you spend yo' money. Don't throw it away, because that's all they is—that's all you goin' to get."

Bully had given five dollars to Daly and five dollars to Cleveland, and a dollar apiece to Tina and Vincent. Hoodoo and Little Suster got fifty cents each. Unca Dempse had taken the six dollars from his pension check and was the first one of the family to be gone up the street.

The old man was a big one for taking in the town on Saturday. He would prowl about until noon, seeking out the remaining old-timers like himself, making small purchases to keep him comfortable during the coming week—more tobacco for his pipe, a pound of coffee in the suspicion that Daly would forget to get any with the groceries, a small tin box of snuff. At noon he would buy some crackers and cheese and go to the wagon to eat his lunch. Then he would take a long drink out of the water jug that stood under the wagon seat and doze in the scant shade in the wagon yard until the rest of the family returned later in the afternoon for the trip home.

Bully had twelve dollars left in his pocket. With the parity check good for fifty dollars, he had paid half of it on his note at the bank.

Always he was mistrustful about going into the cool, dark interior of the bank. The place smelled of money and left him uneasy. The tellers behind their iron-barred cages, with the lights shining down on the counters before them, seemed scarcely human to him, although he had hunted with one or another of them at various times when the white men would come out to the lowlands along the river in the wintertime, seeking the best spots to find rabbits or to build duckblinds. Then they were men nearly like himself, and he could talk to them, laugh with them, and drink a paper cup full of their whisky when they offered it to him. But in the bank, sitting on their high stools behind the barred windows, the green celluloid eyeshades pulled down over their foreheads, they were creatures so totally removed from his own world that Bully found it hard even to look up at them, for fear they would speak to him and he would have to answer back.

He had ducked his head and sidled past the tellers' cages when he went toward the back of the lobby to knock on the door to the cashier's office. With Lester Dewey, Bully was slightly more at ease, since he had dealt directly with the white man for years, coming regularly to the bank in the fall to pay on his note after the cotton was sold, and just as regularly returning in the spring to make his mark on more papers securing a loan that made it possible for him to get another crop planted.

But still Bully sat undecidedly on the forward edge of the chair in the cashier's office. He fumbled with his check, a little hesitant about handing it over, a little doubtful about being forward or about making any move before being asked to by the white man.

"How I stand, Mr. Lester?" he asked, bobbing his head as he spoke. "How I stand now with my note?"

The bank cashier stood up and moved to a shelf where the loan-and-discount ledger lay. He thumbed through the book to find Bully's account. "You're knocking it down, Bully," he turned to say. "Five hundred and fifteen dollars, including the interest since last October."

Bully shook his head slowly. He twisted his hat in his hands, unconsciously crushing a corner of the check as he did so. "Lawd God," he said. "That sound big. That sound like a lot of money, and it go so fast."

Dewey laughed. "It is pretty big, Bully," he said. "And there's not many men like you can borrow that much from us; but you've always paid it off when your crop came in."

Bully nodded. "I pay when I sell the cotton; when I make the crop I pay, even if I do have to borrow it back again." He ran a hand over the short-haired, smooth top of his head, holding the hat by its brim between thumb and forefinger while he scratched at his scalp with the other fingers. He chuckled shortly and tongued his tobacco chew to the other side of his mouth before leaning forward to spit into the brass cuspidor that the cashier kept at the side of his desk. "Lawd, Mr. Lester, it look like I'm bound to make that crop. If I didn't make no cotton I don't know how else I'd pay that note." He still sat uncomfortably on the front edge of the chair.

The cashier smiled with him, not making any comment, and then the white man reached out for the check. "You want to pay some today, Bully?" he asked.

"Yassuh," Bully said, as if the thought had only that minute occurred to him. "My gov'ment check come today, and I like to put half of it on the note. That ought to help some."

"It'll help," the cashier said. "I guess you want the rest of it in cash." He wrote Bully's name across the back of the check, leaving a space for Bully to mark his X. Then he handed the pen to Bully. The cashier called two of the bookkeepers back to watch Bully make his mark. They signed as witnesses; then Dewey took the check off to get the twenty-five dollars in cash and make out a receipt for the note payment.

Bully was standing when the cashier returned. "Thank you, Mr. Lester." He nodded, pocketing the money that had been counted into his palm. "I needed this cash money. I got wages to pay off, I got clothes and groceries to buy; but it look like I just had to come in here and pay some on that note."

"You did right, Bully. It'll make it easier on you in the fall."

Bully backed out the door, still holding his hat in his hands. "I see you then, Mr. Lester," he said. "I see you again when I gathers my crop."

Bully's dependence on the bank was not unusual, though the fact that he had land set him apart and made it possible for him to make a note for an amount larger than the average loan put out to croppers, renters, and the small bottom-land farmers. Title to the land was in Dempse's name, and though Bully had given money to the old man and still was paying him a little at a time, the land belonged to Dempse. "The place will go to you-all when I die," Dempse had said, speaking to Daly and Bully. "Ain't no more than heard from them other chillun since they left; they don't need the place."

For all practical purposes Bully owned the land now. He headed the family and saw that the place was worked. He dealt with the bank. Dempse had signed the notes up until a couple of years ago, but Bully's mark was sufficient now.

The old man would have been in bad shape were it not for Bully and Daly and the rest of the family. His living depended on the family. The monthly pension check would not take care of his needs—nor would the pension check tend to his cooking and his bed and his clothes. The old man had known what he was doing when he asked Bully and Daly to move out there on the place soon after they were married.

Bully depended on the family as much as did Unca Dempse. Just as he needed the loan from the bank to buy seed for planting, so he needed the children to get the crop gathered. Unca Dempse was becoming feeble; he was too childish to do more than an occasional piddling bit of work which in reality came to more hindrance than help. But Daly, Cleveland, Vincent, Tina, Hoodoo, and Little Suster supplied the labor by which the farm was worked.

Bully could not have hired outside help and still made the farming give them a living. The place was too small to demand more labor than the family could furnish, though there were times when the cotton was full open and the threat of rain was growing when the addition of a couple of pickers became necessary. Even at these times Bully hated to have to take on the outside help. When he paid off, it was money going outside the family. It cut down by that much the margin of clear money he would make from the crop and have available for starting another in the following year.

The bank considered Bully a good risk. His ability as a

farmer was known, and several times the county agent had brought men out to look at his crops. Once, following a good spring, when the yield of syrup from his acre of sugar cane had been exceptional, there was mention of it in the column that the county agent wrote for the newspaper in town, and Bully, though he could not read it, treasured the copy of the paper given him by the county agent and stored it away between the pages of the large Bible that lay on a shelf in the house. There had been more syrup than the family could use that year, and Bully had sold five gallons of it in town. The extra money went for fancy groceries, for meat and fruit—and Vincent, for once, had his fill of eating during the following three days.

His note at the bank set Bully apart as much as his controlling the land. He was neither a tenant nor a day hand. His crop, his livestock, his implements were considered security enough by the bank for loans totaling five hundred dollars and more a year. The bank gambled with Bully on the river. The white men knew that if a flood drowned out his crop he would have to come to them for more money to see him through; but still he was a good risk and his security was enough. They knew, and Bully did also, though he could not clearly have put it into words, that it was the family which made him a good risk. The family was large enough to work the place, and Bully got a full share of work out of each of his children. He felt his position as head of the group. Though his affection went deep, his rules were strict, and he never hesitated to whip the children when he figured they needed it. There was something automatic about the way Bully directed all the efforts of his family toward the comfort and security of the whole group. There was no saving up to secure advantage for any one particular member of the family; the work was for the family, not Daly, not Cleveland, not Tina. Let them tear loose in town on Saturday. They could do as they pleased then, but during the week every one of them was going to be there in the field, working, making the crop.

And still, with that, Bully was tolerant. He was tremendously tolerant for a man whose world was bound within the circle of a few miles, whose world centered in the farm and had its farthest limits in the town and the still remembered huge farms along the Brazos. He was tolerant, but not easy. What he saw as right he did, and the children did as he said or else they suffered.

Daly found seldom cause to argue with her husband. In all the years of their marriage there had been no fights, and little quarreling. She defended the children, and if she figured Bully was too harsh, or if she felt that he worked them too hard or attempted to work them when they were truly ill, then her tongue was sharp and her words trimmed Bully down to a size she could handle. Handle him she would, for there was no fear of him in her. Bully was hardheaded, perhaps a little overly cautious, but Daly understood him and trimmed him down when the need came. Bully managed the fields; she managed the house. Their division of control was sound; they ruled together, and the family was strong.

In front of the bank Bully stood with Hoodoo by his side. Vincent had pocketed his money and drifted into the crowd to walk the streets in his own way.

"It's you and me, Hoodoo," Bully said. "Look like everybody else done gone off and left us, so we might as well have us a time."

"I wants to get me a mouth harp, Papa," Hoodoo said. "Let's go to the sto' where I can spend my money for a mouth harp."

Bully took the boy by the hand. "Come on," he said, "else you get lost from me in the crowd. Lawd God, I never seen so many people in town on one day."

The rain waited until one o'clock in the afternoon to start falling. Then it cut loose all of a sudden. A black cloud came up out of the west and the wind blew hard, and within five minutes the streets were running with water. The people crowded together under awnings at the store fronts. The lookers and the walkers surged together to get out of the rain, but they got wet anyhow.

"It ain't goin' to slack up much more," Bully said about three o'clock, and he rounded up Daly and the children and went back to the wagon. Vincent went down on Railroad Street and found Cleveland in a café with Ruby Lee, and Unca Dempse came out of the grocery store when he saw Bully hooking the team to the wagon.

The rain slowed and checked later in the evening, when they were over halfway home, but the road was muddy. The mud dragged at the mules' feet and the team walked slowly. In the bottoms the black mud balled up on the rims of the wagon wheels, and the mules strained against their collars.

Just before sunset there was a slight break in the clouds where the sun shone through for a moment, with the clouds reflecting a yellow light that made the rain-bright trees to either side of the road shine with a strange green brilliance. But by the time the wagon was crossing Spring Creek the clouds had closed in again, and it was dark and raining when Bully unhooked the team in the lot.

The two mules moved into the shelter of the barn. Ear-spraddled, sore-shouldered, and wet, they stood before the corn boxes, stood under the chicken roosts while drip water dripped through the roof. The wind came up again to blow strong and loud while rain beat under the eaves. The yellow evening light had darked into black night, and the two mules nickered, nuzzled for corn, slobbered the ears, and spilled grains to the mud; the rooster and hens fluttered on the perch bars and dropped their droppings on the backs of the mules—dropped their droppings, too wet, too settled to do else but flutter and quarrel, leaving the spilled grains to lie and be stomped into the mud of the barn floor. The mules stood weary, mud-splashed, in the barn, rain-wet and chicken-spotted alike, and waited for the night to pass.

CHAPTER SEVEN

Cul Sally went toward his own field, where his wife waited with her hoe and grasped the check rein on Cul's team to keep the mules standing. Cul left Cleveland to follow his blue mule and his Pete mule and his cultivator. Cul was a little hurt. He had known Cleveland a long time; they had cut wood together, and now on John Chaney's place on the Brazos the fields that they were working for the white man lay side by side.

"Cleveland so damn closemouthed," Cul said to his wife. "No wonder he always havin' people pick trouble with him. He swell up like a frog and look like he just as soon hit you side the head as talk to you."

Cleveland was in no mood for talking. He was intent on watching how the cultivator feet ran. When he was working he could keep his mind on his cotton, and keep busy with watching how the team walked and with seeing that he plowed close enough to the plants without covering them or cutting them up. He could forget about tangling with Buddy Boy on the turnrow and forget about the white man in his truck.

The field was broad. The far turnrow was along a tree-lined creek that ran through the red bottom land to the river. The rows were long and straight. The land was flat. Straight down the cotton rows to the west, beyond the creek that ran diagonally across Cleveland's line of vision, was the Brazos, rolling between its high banks and cutting a wide gash in the rich red land of the flood plain. The river curved in a huge meander, and the creek joined it to the south, and the creek and the river were like tentacles that reached out through the country, cradling the fertile land, holding in the compass of tremendous arms the fields, the crops, the houses, and the people that were all a part of the bottom land.

The land from the creek bank that bounded the far end of

Cleveland's field and south to where the curving river was crossed by the highway was John Chaney's. The river farm was bounded by the creek and the river and the highway, and on the east, in the higher ground, the boundary was a surveyor's line. The headquarters buildings stood near the middle of the wide fields. The roads and the turnrows spread out from the central lots and barns past the houses where the third-and-fourth hands lived, past the tall corn and the green cotton, past the oats and the sorghum. John Chaney kept his tractors, with their harrows and gang plows, at the big barns of the headquarters, and the day hands had their houses there close to the commissary; but the families working the smaller sections of land for the white man had their own cultivators and their own teams, and they made their crops for John Chaney with what he considered a minimum of supervision.

Cleveland would just as soon do without the supervision altogether. He knew how to farm, and as long as he felt that it was his crop he was going to work it right and make something out of it. He spoke to the mules, he swung the rope lines against their sides to make them step faster while the morning was still cool. Later in the day, as the sun rose higher, the mules would walk more slowly. By dinnertime their sides would be heaving; salty foam would have worked up under the collar pads and between their legs.

Cleveland made a round and was back on the turnrow when he saw Ruby Lee coming down the road. She was even with the cornfield. From where he stood, Cleveland could see only the roof of the house. The tall corn cut off his vision. Ruby Lee had no hoe with her, and he wondered at it until he remembered what she had said about going to the store. Every day she had her cleaning to do at the house. There had been a small washing to get out; she had to go to the well after water; and this morning she claimed she had to take off to go to the store. Had it not been for all that she would have been with him when Buddy Boy started talking, and then Ruby Lee would have known howcome he was late coming home last night.

She would have known part of it, the part that had to do with Lometa and Lometa's house, but she would not have known it all. Cleveland lacked complete understanding of it all himself; he did not know why it was he took off down the road after putting the mules in the barn. It looked like he just had to get out and walk the road, and first thing he knew he was going toward Lometa's house.

Ruby Lee was swinging the water jug in her hand. The gallon jug was wrapped with tow-sacking which had been dampened so that evaporation would keep the water cool. "You forgot this," Ruby Lee said as she came close enough to lift the jug toward Cleveland. "You got off in too big a hurry and left it there in the kitchen."

Cleveland took the jug from her and pulled out the stopper. He took a long drink before going to the off side of the Pete mule to sling the jug from the hame by the leather strap through the handle. "I put it in the shade when I get to the other end of the field," Cleveland said. "You goin' on to the sto' now?"

Ruby Lee had on shoes. Her hair was pinned up. She had not worked long with it, as she would for going to town on Saturday, but it was neat and she had it pulled up off her neck and wound into two buns that rested on either side of her head just behind her ears. She wore a print cotton dress; it was one of her good dresses.

"I got a little more to do at the house," she said. "I saw yo' water jug in the kitchen and come on down here to bring it because I knew you'd be gettin' thirsty."

"I hope you get back," Cleveland said. "I hope you get on back here and come to the field. This cotton need walkin' through with a hoe if we goin' to keep it out the grass."

"I aim to come to the field after dinner." Ruby Lee stepped back to the harder dirt of the turnrow so that the loose plowed earth between the cotton rows would not get into her shoes. "I aim to get on up there and get back and have dinner ready, and I bring my hoe to the field this e'nin'."

"I may not come to the house," Cleveland said. "I might keep on goin' here and try to get caught up. If we get caught up I was goin' to ask Mr. John again to let me go. We get the crop ready to lay by and maybe he say it's all right to leave here for a couple of days."

It was not so much what he said as the way he said it that made Ruby Lee feel guilty about not coming to the field. "I aimed to tell you last night," she said. "If I could have talked with you I'd have told you I had to come to the sto'."

"Go on," Cleveland said. "We got to have groceries in the house. But I just say that if we get the crop laid by the white man might let us leave here for a couple of days."

"Did you ask him again? Did he tell you no, and that's what made you mad since Sadday?"

"You know we didn't see Papa and them in town," Cleveland said, not looking at his wife. He dug into his shirt pocket for the sack of tobacco and the cigarette papers, and looked at his hands as he made his cigarette. Lately he was finding it harder and harder to look her in the eye when he talked to her, no matter what it was he had to say to her. He could not joke with her, and it was only under the drive of sudden and burning anger that his eyes looked into hers.

"You know I worried about Papa and them," he said now, deliberately, as if explaining something to a child. "Since that mule died they ain't had no way to get in to town without walkin'. Papa been had to borrow a mule when he could to make a little crop, and you know I want to get out there and see do they need me."

Ruby Lee stepped closer. This was the first time in days that Cleveland had said to her what was on his mind, and unconsciously she made the move toward him. "I know," she said. "I know you want to go. But what could you do? How you goin' to leave this crop long enough to help out any?"

"I got these mules." Cleveland looked at the ground, as if he knew that his figuring was no good but had to figure nevertheless. "If I could get these mules back there I could get that place cleaned up. I could get it out the grass."

"They yo' mules, Clevelan'," Ruby Lee said. "You bought them mules and paid for them."

"Sho'!" Cleveland's eyes were wide as he raised his head. His eyes stood out white under the shadow of his hatbrim, except for the dark iris and the pupil which was small from the brightness of the sun on the dry dust of the turnrow. "They my mules. Why can't I take them where I want to? This my crop, too. I make it for the man; he don't have to tell me how to make it. Why can't I go when I want to? It don't take me long to go out yonder and see how Papa and them makin' out."

"We third-and-fourth hands, Clevelan'," Ruby Lee reminded him. "You own the mules, but the land belong to Mr. John, and the house belong to him. It look like if we want to stay and make a crop we got to do what he say."

Cleveland struck a match to the cigarette. He flipped the match to the ground and stepped on it.

"Us been here nearly a year," he said. He drew deep on the cigarette and held the smoke in his lungs before jetting it out through his nostrils. "Us been here in these bottoms nearly a year, and it look like already us belong to the man. I come out here to make a crop and get some money so us could work toward gettin' a place for ourselves. We worked last summer choppin' and then in the fall we went to pickin' cotton, and not until wintertime did Mr. John let us move on this place. He ain't let us alone since then. I wish he wouldn't come 'round there to the house; I wish he let me do my own farmin'."

"The place his," Ruby Lee said. "It look like us got to do what he say."

Cleveland looked at her from under the brim of his hat. He looked at her dress and at her hair. Sometimes he wished she were not quite so well-shaped and so pretty. Maybe then he would not have so much reason to worry about her. And he wished she were not quite so afraid to have them do something for themselves. She'd been in the bottoms too long; her folks had worked for the white man for too long. Sometimes it looked to Cleveland as if working for the white man and doing what he said were the only thing she knew. With Bully, on the place on the Navasot', it had not been like that. The work there was their own, and all of what they made they kept.

Bully drove him harder than the white man ever had, but Bully was his father and had a right to make him work hard. That kind of work never did hurt Cleveland, and he knew it, though he would try to talk back to Bully at times and grumble about having to go out in the heat of the day; but the work was for the family, and Bully was his father. That kind of work, it seemed to Cleveland, was right.

"We got to do what Mr. John say," Cleveland said slowly. "But not everything he say. We workin' for us as much as we workin' for him, and I wish you remember that." He threw down his cigarette and stomped on it. He turned back to the cultivator and placed the lines around his neck again.

"Go on to the sto', Ruby Lee," he said. "You get hot and sweat yo' dress out if you wait. Go on to the sto' and see if the white man there to tell you anything. I seen him head that way when he left here a while ago."

Ruby Lee need not have known anything about the fight this morning if she were not going to the store. Cleveland knew that from the house she could not have seen the fight. But the story would have made its way to the headquarters by now; somebody would have come in and told about Cleveland and Buddy Boy tangling with each other over Lometa.

"Go on to the sto'," Cleveland said. "I ain't got time to stand here and talk. You get on up there and get back so you can bring yo' hoe to the field. We got to get this crop clean; the white man say we got to get this crop clean."

CHAPTER EIGHT

Hoodoo got up and went to the window to look out at the gray morning. "Wake up, Little Suster," he said. "Come here to the window and look at the rain. Come look at the water that stand on the ground."

Little Suster turned on her pallet and stretched. She sat up yawning and kept herself under the covers because the air inside the house was damp and cold. The room was clammy and close with all the windows and doors shut, and the leak water splashing into the pan knocked droplets out to wet the floor in a circle about the pan.

"I thought the rain had stopped," she said. She got to her feet, wrapping the quilt from her pallet around her as she came across the room, circling to avoid the wet area around the pan under the leak.

"It woke me up." Hoodoo had his face close to the window glass. "It come on again all of a sudden and it woke me up. Look out there, Little Suster—look out there at the yard. Look at them trees across the road. It's all you can do to see them, and they just there across the road."

"Ha' mercy," Little Suster said, imitating Daly's voice. "It's solid water. Listen to it on the roof—I can't hardly hear you talk."

"I'm goin' out," Hoodoo said. "I'm goin' to run out in the yard and wade while it still rainin'." He started for the door that led to the room where Bully and Daly slept, but he had talked too loudly, and Bully was awake.

"You stay in this house," Bully ordered. "You open that door and run out and I make you stay out there all day. Don't you go out there and get wet and come trackin' mud and water in here. You-all get on back in there and lie down. You have yo' mama awake in a minute."

"I'm awake now," Daly said beside him. "Can't nobody sleep with all this noise and rain on the roof. Somebody got to get up and empty the water out of them pans before they run over. Get up, Bully, and empty the pans."

"Hoodoo," Bully said, "go yonder in the kitchen and empty them pans for yo' mama. Pour the water out the back door—but you go out to run in the yard before breakfast and I whip you from now to dinnertime."

"Help him, Little Suster," Daly said. "And then you-all get back to bed. We can't work today, we might as well lie here and rest."

"I got to get up," Bully said, yawning. "Me and Cleveland got to get out and look for that cow. We got to start on soon as this rain slack." He sat up and swung his feet over the side of the bed. Half the buttons on his undershirt had come undone while he slept, and he fumbled at them with one hand while he rubbed his face with the other. He felt under the bed for his shoes while he looked toward the window, gray with the morning light and the rain beyond. "You might as well go on fix some breakfast now," he said to Daly, speaking over his shoulder. He gaped. "This rain just come up; it might slack off again just as quick."

Daly got out of bed then and went to the wall, where a faded wrapper hung from a nail. Daly was far from fat; her gown was loose on her figure. She was large in breast and hips and stout in the waist, but her flesh was firm. The work in the field and in the house kept her hard, and though she was big she carried herself well. She could dress to look good when she had the clothes for it, and even now, this early in the morning, and it rainy, she could have made Bully sweet-talk to her had she not known that he was worried about the rain and the cow, and had she not been worried about them herself. She slipped her brown arms into the sleeves of the wrapper and tied the belt around her waist. For slippers she put on a pair of Bully's field shoes that stood dry behind the door.

They felt the cold draft blowing in from the kitchen, where Hoodoo and Little Suster were emptying the drip pans out the door. "Lawd God," Daly said, going to the kitchen to look out over the flooded back yard. "Where Cleveland been in all this water?"

Bully came up behind her and looked over Daly's shoulder to see Cleveland come splashing across the yard from the barn lot. The water in the back yard was halfway up to the top of Cleveland's shoes. He was running, and the water he knocked up wet the breeches legs that he had rolled up to a point just below his knees. His muscled brown legs were mud-spotted.

He shook himself as he came in the kitchen door, sending drops of water flying through the air as a dog would. The rain was cold; it had Cleveland wide-awake; it had him dripping on Daly's clean kitchen floor. Water squished out over his shoe-tops.

"Hanh!" he grunted, raking a hand downward from his hairline to the tip of his nose and slinging the drops against the wall. "Papa, I thought the cow might have come up, but she ain't in the barn yet. She ain't in the pastuh neither." He snorted, blowing at the water that rolled in drops from his hairline to the tip of his nose.

"Get out of here," Daly said. "Go change them clothes. You messin' up my kitchen."

"You can't see to the far end of the pastuh," Bully said. "Maybe she come back and is down there under some tree."

Cleveland shook his head. "She would have come to the barn. I went out and looked for her, but I couldn't see her nowhere."

About the only name the bobtailed Jersey had ever heard was "Cow," and she would never answer to that. "Go down in the pastuh and bring up the cow, Hoodoo," Bully would shout from the edge of the field when the sun began to get low in the west.

"Vincent got to milk that cow this e'nin'," Tina would say.

"I done milked for the last two days. Howcome Cleveland and Vincent don't go out there to the barn and milk that cow?"

The cow paid no attention to Hoodoo when he came running and yelling down through the little pasture. Two black spots alongside her backbone in front of the hipbones made her appear thin and gaunt. The knobby hips seemed ready to break out through her skin. But she had a good bit of meat on her and gave two gallons of milk a day on the days that the eight-months-old calf did not slip through the lot fence and get to her to suck her dry before Hoodoo could bring her to the barn for milking. Hoodoo would shout and run toward her, waving his arms, but she would do no more than raise her head from the grass to look at him before reaching back to lick at the flies on her flanks. That shortened, brushless tail did little to help her, and the horn flies gathered in swarms on her sides and belly and worried her all day.

Bully had cut the tail short while she was still a heifer, after she got worms in a barbed-wire cut during the summer. Bully tried doctoring her with Dr. LeGear's powders and with cresylic ointment and with axle grease, but the flies kept bothering her and she kept swinging her tail at them and keeping the sore open, and one day when she kicked Bully in the groin while he was trying to doctor her he called for Cleveland to come and throw the heifer. As soon as Bully was able to stand up straight he took the ax and cut her tail off above the running sore.

They took a rag and daubed it with axle grease and tied a bandage over the end of the heifer's tail, and in less than a week the place had scabbed over and was healing. By the end of two months flesh was growing back over the end of the bone, and her tail was well again. But she did not have any long brush of brown hair to drag the ground and get full of mud and cocklebures. She had no way to swing at the flies that lit on her back and sides, and bending back her neck only let her lick at those settled on the under part of her belly. She got right bony before the frost and cold weather came to drive away the horn flies that first year her tail was off, and Bully looked at her in the pasture and worried.

"That heifer don't get no chance to eat for kickin' at them flies," he said. "That goin' to be the runninest cow they is this side of the river. You can't drive her out of no brush thicket in the middle of the day, and she jump any fence in this country when the flies get at her."

"You ought to put a forked stick on that heifer's neck," Daly said after the coming four-year-old had broken into her garden and eaten down half the collards. "She won't get through no fence if you put a stick on her neck."

"I go cut a stick, Papa," Cleveland offered. "I know where they a forked ellum growin' down there close to the turnrow. She won't break no fence when I finish with her."

"We goin' to leave that cow alone," Bully said. "I done nearly ruined that cow when I cut her tail off short, and if she got a stick on her head she can't get at them flies on her back. Them flies drive that cow crazy if she can't lick at them. She won't give no milk, and them chillun need to have they milk. We goin' to leave that cow alone. We done done enough damage to her already."

The cow paid Hoodoo no mind when he came to the pasture to drive her up for milking. If the calf was bawling in the lot, that was no bother to the cow. If she was not through eating and ready to go to the barn lot she wouldn't go. Hoodoo took to carrying a stick with him, or a dry cornstalk, and he'd walk up to the Jersey and beat her on the flanks to start her toward the barn. But the cow kept on eating.

Cleveland watched Hoodoo from the back yard and near rolled on the ground with laughing. "Hit her some mo', Hoodoo," he called. "She like for you to hit her with that cornstalk. You drivin' the flies away."

When she was ready, she would come to the barn and let the calf suck, and stand quietly to let Tina or Vincent milk her. She would let Hoodoo come up to her and scratch her between the hind legs with a corncob to ease the itching spots where the ticks clung and where the flies had feasted until they brought blood which scaled off in dry specks under Hoodoo's scratching.

She didn't care what they called her. It was all right with her. "Cow" was as good as anything. When she got ready to go she was going; when she didn't want her calf around she would have nothing to do with it. She would butt a calf away from her while it was sucking, and when it tried to come back she would kick it slap in the ribs until it was weaned for a day anyhow. When she was bulling there was no fence high enough to begin to hold her. If she could not go over the fence she would find a soft post and put her head through the wires and start walking. The staples spanged out and the wires parted and the cow was on the other side. Or if there was no place to go through a fence she would look for a water gap and go under. When the season came on her and she was in heat she was ready to go.

Ugly-looking, black-faced, bobtailed little muley that she was, she always seemed to have a liking for the best bull in the country, and she would head straight for John Chaney's pasture two miles up the Navasot', where the white man kept a herd of whitefaces fattening on the thick mesquite grass. Every time the cow came in heat and they missed her, Bully and Cleveland would take off down the road and head for the white man's pasture, and there would be that black-spotted cow cropping mesquite grass with Mr. John's fat Herefords. And just as regular as clockwork, nine months later she would throw a big-eyed, white-faced red calf, pretty as a picture, good-boned and sturdy. Since Bully raised the heifer she had brought three calves, and every time she came in fresh again and her milk cleared up she gave a regular two gallons a day, plenty for Daly to use in cooking and put on the table for them to drink clabbered, and every now and then there would be enough sour cream skimmed off and saved for them to make butter.

"We goin' to leave that cow alone," Bully said. "We ain't goin' to put no stick on that cow's neck. Look yonder how she don't pay no mind to Hoodoo when he go to drive her up. That cow smart; she know her own mind, and I ain't goin' to waste no time puttin' a stick on her neck when she have it left hangin' on a fence post the next mornin'."

The cow had a stick on her neck now; she had one that wouldn't come off, and it kept her in one place, but it didn't help Bully and Cleveland to find her.

The rain kept on. It fell all day and off and on for another night. For a week it seemed to rain solid, and although there were times when the sun did shine through for a few hours or a half-day at a time, the rain was remembered and the sun forgot.

The rolling creeks fed water into the river and the river swelled. All along its course the runoff crowded into the channel, and the channel was too small to hold the water. The big Brazos was bank-full also, and when the Navasot' crest hit the Brazos it started backing up, and the water in the bottoms turned from dirty gray to red. The red waters spread over the black land and swirled slowly among the lower branches of the pecan trees and the elms and the willows. The yaupon thickets barely thrust their tops above the flood.

And six feet above the banks of a slough that ran back into John Chaney's pasture, the bobtailed, black-faced cow floated with her neck caught in the fork of a young elm. Her head was submerged, held there by the tree fork, but her body floated high in the water. She was on her right side. Her four legs stuck out stiffly; her belly was puffed up round and tight; and she swung back and forth, hanging by her neck, as the slow flood currents tugged at her.

She had a stick on her neck now. The river put it there somehow when the currents brought her up against the elm tree two days ago. If the water's pull were not too strong, and if the flesh and bone of her neck held out, she would be there when the river slid back between its banks. But it was hard to tell how long she would hang on. Her belly was mighty tight, and the green flies were all over her high side, getting in their work before the buzzards could find her down there under the thicket of branches.

CHAPTER NINE

"I don't know how my dog got hurt," Joe Coby said. Joe had on a flat-crowned felt hat with a brim that was limp in the back. He had on clean overalls and a neat shirt that had all the buttons on it. Joe Coby walked lightly; it hardly seemed possible that he could get any dirt in his shoes when he followed the plow. He had a light brown skin and a sharp face. He was well-built, had strong shoulders; but he was slim, his hips were narrow, and he was annoyingly careful in his manner. He was ten years older than Cleveland.

"That dog was limpin' this mornin'," Joe said. "It look like a truck run over him or a mule kicked him. I don't know when it happen—he was all right yestiddy."

Cleveland grunted while he looked at Joe Coby, trying to figure out whether Joe had seen him walking the road by his house last night. "Yo' dog run around a lot," he said. "It's a wonder he ain't been killed long before now."

Joe Coby bristled. "That dog all right," he said. "He a good watchdog to stay there at home when I'm in the field. He don't do no harm; if he bark and raise hell sometime it's because he's a dog."

Joe was standing on the turnrow only a few yards below the spot where Ruby Lee had been earlier. The sun was rising higher in the sky, getting on toward noon, and Cleveland had made a good start on the field. A broad strip of the fresh-turned earth, laced with the straight lines of green cotton, lay between him and the edge of the corn. He was resting the mules at the turnrow, letting them blow and cool off, when Joe Coby came down the road with his hoe over his shoulder.

"You quittin' early," Cleveland had said. "Howcome you goin' in before dinnertime?"

"We done caught up." Joe Coby spoke proudly, and pulled a clean white handkerchief out of his hip pocket to wipe at his face. He put the hoe down on the ground with the long handle leaning back against his shoulder, and used the handkerchief to wipe his hands. The way he carried the hoe and handled it made it seem that he was trying to keep from raising callouses on his hands. In spite of his careful show of fastidiousness, Joe was good on a farm. He worked hard and his hands were tough, but he walked like he wanted it known that he never sweat.

"Me and my wife finished that field this mornin'. We didn't have much more to do." Joe was unhurried, leisurely, as he leaned on the hoe handle and watched Cleveland break a cultivator foot from the ground and clean the gummed dirt from the small sweep. "I guess I have to get back in there next week and walk through it once more, but we done just about laid by. Tomorrow we goin' to start some day labor for Mr. John. He's done said he want me and my wife over there to help him get out of the grass."

"What you goin' to do today?" Cleveland had little interest in how Joe Coby was doing with his crop, but it was all right to have somebody to talk to while the mules were resting. "You goin' to lay off this e'nin' and stay in the shade?"

"I don't know," Joe Coby said. "We might take off and go in to town if we can find a ride. Now that we caught up it look like I just as soon go in to town for a little while. You ought to get through, Clevelan'. You ought to make them mules step out so you get done and have you a day's rest."

"Look at them mules," Cleveland grunted. "You know I can't run them mules in this hot sun. They good, but I got to take it slow with them, else they goin' to fall out."

Joe Coby laughed at him. "You too easy with that team," he said. "You ought to make them step out, and then you get yo' crop made." He came a little closer and leaned forward, speaking to Cleveland with great secrecy although there were no others to hear. "I been out here longer than you, and I know these bottoms and I know Mr. John. That white man like to see a team workin' in the field; he don't like to see them stand and blow on the turnrow. Why don't you get you some good mules, Clevelan'?"

Cleveland hunched his shoulders slowly. His head started to draw down like a turtle's, and his lips began to press against each other, puckering outward. "Look here, Joe Coby," Cleveland growled, "I work this crop like I want to. I work my mules like I want to. I been had this team—I damn near been raised up with these mules—and I know how they work. The less the white man try to tell me how to do, the less you try to tell me how to do, the better it goin' to be."

"Hold on, Clevelan'. Hold on, I don't mean to try to tell you how to do. I just talkin' and tell you what I thought. First thing you know you jump me like you did Buddy Boy."

Cleveland looked at Joe as if he had been been planning to do just that and was still considering the idea. Then Cleveland grinned slowly. Joe Coby standing there in his fresh clothes, in his clean shirt, talking fast to cover up for getting into what was not his business, struck Cleveland as funny. "Don't run, Joe," Cleveland said, laughing more to himself than at Joe Coby. "I won't jump on you. I won't mess up them clothes by rollin' you in the dirt."

Cleveland could not say why it was he disliked the smaller, light-skinned man. Joe Coby had never done him any wrong, but Cleveland cared little for his neighbor. Joe Coby's house stood hardly more than a half-mile away from Cleveland's, yet

Joe and his wife had not been down to visit with Cleveland and Ruby Lee in all the time since the younger couple had moved there. There was a jealousy in Joe that Cleveland sensed; an almost indefinable atmosphere of suspicion, guile, and general insincerity emanated from Joe's neat person and bred distrust in Cleveland, a distrust that grew along with a feeling of physical superiority and unexpressed antagonism.

Joe Coby's manner might have been born of an insecurity that had its basis in a number of causes, but the latest cause was clear and definite—the white man's dealing with Cleveland. Joe had been on his present place for a long time, and John Chaney had kept him there without offering to let him move when Walter Steptoe left the house and the land that Cleveland had now. Walter started driving truck for the white man and moved his family into a house up at the headquarters, and that left idle the farm on the creek. Chaney might have offered the place to Joe Coby first, giving him the refusal of it, but the white man said nothing to Joe and moved Cleveland in there during the fall.

Joe Coby's land was as good as that held by Cleveland; the two places were separated by only the width of Cul Sally's fields, but Joe's land lay farther down the creek away from the highway that led to town. The house that Cleveland was in was a little tighter, but the repairs had been made by Cleveland during the winter after he moved in. Cleveland's house was larger; it had one more room than Joe's, and that was all the difference. But it was a difference that meant something to Joe Coby. He had been with John Chaney a long time and he figured he was due to get the best that there was coming.

It was hard to say why the white man had given Cleveland preference. Most likely he had not thought that preference was involved. Joe Coby was a good farmer, he had been on the same place for a long time and made a good crop there every year; Cleveland was young and strong, able to whip out the Johnson grass and the vines that had started creeping from the creek bank into the fields during the last year that Walter Steptoe fooled with the place. Most likely that was all there was to it, and the white man put Cleveland in there to try him out, to see how he would do.

But Joe Coby could not see it that way. Cleveland had got ahead of him someway, and he resented the younger man's strength and his ability to take that team of old wornout mules and make headway in the tough, flat land along the creek.

Cleveland and Ruby Lee had done well through the fall and winter. They had been married but five months when they moved into the house, and they worked hard at getting the place into livable condition. The high water came up in the winter and the following spring, but they did not let it bother them. They let it climb up the banks of the deep-cut creek and flood out into the low flats and sloughs, and they did not worry about the river. They felt big enough to stand against the Brazos and ride it out, because they had a place of their own and the white man had told Cleveland he was going to give him a chance to make a crop there.

It might have been Joe Coby's wife that kept Joe from being too good a neighbor. Somehow Lula could not get along with Ruby Lee, and Lula started talking to Joe about it at night.

"That girl switch around like she own these bottoms," Lula said. "She get mighty smart when she go to town on Sadday. She pull that hair up on her head and wear them tight dresses and walk the streets like the place hers and they ain't nobody else can dress up to look as good as she does." Lula ought not to have worried about Ruby Lee. The girl was not a source of competition, and Lula had managed to keep her looks pretty well for her age, which was thirty-seven. She was two years older than Joe, and he was her third husband. There were no children. She had never worked in the fields too long and too hard, and her figure was still good. She never lacked for men to come up and talk to her in town, but when Ruby Lee and

Cleveland moved onto the place she started talking against the girl.

"They ain't been married more than six months," Lula said, sitting on the front porch at night with Joe, "and I bet that girl done made a fool out of Clevelan' so many times he couldn't count them if he knew."

It was interesting to Joe; he had watched Ruby Lee when she came to the field to bring water to Cleveland when he was breaking the ground to get it ready for planting. But he knew better than to go down there and try to talk to her when Cleveland was anywhere within five miles of the place, and he knew better, too, than to try slipping off down there without Lula's finding out about it.

"I don't know," he said, drawing on a ready-made cigarette that he had taken from the pack in his shirt pocket. "I never heard nothin' said against her. I never heard tell of Ruby Lee carryin' on with anybody."

"You a fool, Joe," his wife said. "I ain't been talkin' about these niggers out here—I ain't been talkin' about these field hands. Ain't you watched how Mr. John always stop by there? Ain't you seen how the white man's truck always pull up down at that house?"

Joe sat up straight in his chair. He had never been in trouble with John Chaney. He never talked about the white man with any of the other tenants. He got along fine by doing just what John Chaney said, and sometimes Lula worried the fool out of him by the way she talked.

"Look here," he said worriedly. "Lula, you ought not to talk like that. Sho', Mr. John stop by there, but Clevelan' a new man; when he got a new hand on his place he want to see him get started right. I don't know what you mean when you talk like that about Mr. John stoppin' his truck down there."

Lula laughed and sat combing her hair straight while her husband lectured her. "You a fool, Joe," she said, but she knew that he was not. She knew Joe Coby well enough to understand that he would speak no word against the white man to anybody, not even to his wife, lest it should get out and get him in trouble. Trouble was one thing that Joe liked to avoid, especially when it was trouble that was likely to keep him from getting ahead. He was no fool, but Lula used the word in speaking to him. It was her one best way of getting under his skin and needling him into quicker action toward getting her what she wanted.

Joe Coby was a smaller man than Cleveland. He lacked the strength that Cleveland had in his broad back and knotted shoulders, but Joe was not weak by any means, and Lula knew that he put up with her only as long as she helped him to get ahead with John Chaney. As long as she managed to stay with Joe she would be all right, because Joe was not going to be left behind when there was something extra to be had.

"You ought to been had that place Clevelan' on," she said. "It don't look right to me that Mr. John move that boy on there when you been with him for so long."

"This place all right," Joe answered. "We managed to make a pretty good crop here." But he could not help feeling that what Lula said was right, and it started showing whenever he passed Cleveland and Ruby Lee on the road, or saw them in town, or stopped for a little while to talk to Cleveland in the field.

Joe stood now on the turnrow where Cleveland had stopped his team, and tried to figure out just how far he could go with talking to Cleveland without making him mad. He wanted to avoid rousing Cleveland too much; the way that boy had climbed onto Buddy Boy at sunup convinced Joe Coby that the last thing he wanted to do was to cross Cleveland openly.

"Some of them say . . ." Joe advanced cautiously. "I was talkin' with Cul Sally and some of them in town Sadday, and they say you talkin' about leavin' Mr. John. You goin' to make this crop out, Clevelan', or you goin' to pull out before you gets it made in the fall?"

Cleveland's head lifted quickly and his eyelids narrowed as he stared at Joe Coby's sharp face. "You ain't heard anybody say that. I ain't said nothin' about aimin' to leave out from here. What the hell you talkin' about, Joe Coby?"

Joe started backing water. "That's just some talk I heard in town. I know they ain't nothin' to it, but I want to ask you. I thought maybe you was goin' back out yonder to the Navasot' to yo' folks' place."

"How I'm goin' to go anywhere when I got this crop to lay by?" Cleveland asked. "And howcome you want to know so bad what I'm goin' to do?" Cleveland had had enough of talking to Joe Coby. He was standing there on the turnrow asking questions and running off at the mouth and taking up time when the team was ready to go again.

"I'm got this field to finish," Cleveland said, turning to take up the lines. "You can stand there if you want to and miss yo' rest, but you goin' to be by yo'self, because I'm got work to do."

CHAPTER TEN

Bully stood by the gap that opened from the pasture to the cornfield. One foot was propped on the lower strand of rusty fence wire, and his upper body leaned toward the fence. His left shoulder was against the gap post, and the forearm was crossed in front of his chest, lying along the top wire. He shifted his arm a little so that the sharp barbs that were twisted into the strand would not prick his skin. His hat, pulled down low over his forehead, shaded his eyes so that he could look without squinting out over the glimmering, sunlighted cornfield.

He had been standing there, shifting position occasionally to make himself comfortable, for a full quarter of an hour, and he continued to look toward the river while the sun rose higher in the sky behind him and grew warm enough to burn with some discomfort through the shirt that was stretched tight across his back and hunched shoulders. He slipped his right hand into the pocket of his overalls and pulled out a wooden match, which he held loosely just back of the head while he chewed the other end into a splayed brush, and then he held the match tighter while his fingers moved it to scrub over his teeth and gums like a snuff brush. He spit small pieces of the chewed match stem and continued to scrub at his teeth even though he heard Cleveland's footsteps and the grass brushing against trousers legs as his son came toward him across the pasture.

Nor did Cleveland speak when he came up to the fence beside his father. He stood silently for a moment, looking also toward the river, and then stepped closer to the fence, crossing his arms to prop himself against it, but leaning lightly, so as not to put too much pressure on the barbed wire.

It was Bully who spoke first. Cleveland had been there at his right side for nearly a minute before Bully took the match stem out of his mouth and said, "I think it's about to come to a standstill. I was down there a while ago, but it don't look to me like it's comin' up any more."

"Unless the Brazos back it up more it ought to start fallin'," Cleveland said.

The wagon tracks that led across the pasture from the barn passed through the gap and bordered the edge of the cornfield, going down the turnrow toward the lowlands where the floodwaters stood now in June, after more than two weeks of slow and steady rising. The rains had stopped in the area drained by the lower reach of the narrow Navasot', where Bully's farm lay, and the rains had stopped out in the wide flood plain of the Brazos, across which the dirty gray Navasot' cut to empty into the bigger red river; but the cloudy weather held on and the rains moved north, falling on the hills and the bottom lands that lay far upstream.

The arms of the river reached far back into the land, and the spreading creeks, the branches, the ditches, the dry-weather gullies—all the network of drainage that was like fingers to the extended arms of the two rivers—caught the runoff from the rain-soaked ground and fed it downstream to swell the flood where the two rivers came together. Creeping out over their banks, the Brazos and the Navasot' met and in the lowlands became one—not rivers, but a lake filled with thick red water and slow, swirling currents, drifting logs, rafts of brush, and dead, floating livestock.

When it was on the rise, the slow, silent floodwater sent feelers out ahead of it, little trickles of water to run up the middles between the cotton rows—trickles that searched out the low ground, dissolved the clods, cut away the heaped earth of the cotton rows until the higher lying clods toppled quietly and fell with hardly a plop into the waiting gray feeler. The water went on, and the middles were filled, the rows covered, and the cotton fields resembled rice paddies. Still the water rose, climbing up the stalks from one branch to another; and the leaves were drowned, and the very tops of the stalks caught and held the light drift of dried grass, old cornstalks, and brushy twigs. Then the tops were under, and the Navasot' water turned red with the backwash from the big river to the west, and in the darkness of the deep floodwater the cotton soured while muddy sediment settled on the leaves; and the water swelled higher while catfish, buffalo, and the long-billed gars rose out of the river channel to swim down the cotton rows and browse slowly through their widened territory.

At standstill the water had more than half an acre of Bully's lower corn flooded. As he stood now by the pasture gap Bully could see where the wagon tracks on the turnrow dipped into the flood at the far side of the field. The morning sun made the water bright; he could see the flood glinting through the lower few rows of the field.

"It might be to a standstill," Bully said. "It look to me like it done quit risin', but I'd hate to be wrong and have it come up and get all that corn. If it do that we done losed about everything."

Cleveland did not move, except to work his jaws for a moment and then spit through his teeth toward a cornstalk at the end of the first row. The corn lacked over a month's growth of full development. The stalks were tall and strong, the leaves broad and dark green, filled with sap and life from the moisture that lay in the ground. The golden tassels swayed a foot and more above the head of either man, but the ears were not yet filled out, and though they were good for table use, they wanted the growth and maturity that would come with the drying heat of later summer.

"Like I say"—Cleveland spoke—"unless the Brazos back up some more it ought to start fallin'."

"But if it don't," Bully reasoned, "we goin' to lose that corn. And I don't know, I don't know but what we ought to go in there and cut them stalks and haul them out. Then we could shock it and let it dry. The mules eat them stalks when they tender; the leaves make good fodder."

Cleveland shook his head. He shifted his arms on the wire fence so that the barbs would have a new place to dig into his skin. "The water ought to fall," he said. "It ought to go down."

Bully was still figuring on how he could get in there and save some of his crop, and he did not turn toward Cleveland or pay much attention to what his son was saying. He talked more to himself than to Cleveland.

"I seen a white man do it," Bully said. "Before I moved up here to this place I seen a white man get his corn out of the water. He went into the field in a boat and cut that corn till he made a load, and then he brought it out till he had a wagonload and carried it to the barn."

"I wouldn't cut the corn," Cleveland said. "I don't believe the water goin' to get any higher, and if we cut that corn and feed it up green there ain't goin' to be anything left. There ain't time to make another crop this summer."

"I know." Bully craned his neck, stretching it to get a crick out of it, and he rubbed his hand over his face and his chin. He had a sparse growth of whiskers, a few hairs on his jaw just in front of his ear lobes, and a few more on his chin. The beard was beginning to gray, and Bully had not shaved for a couple of days. The hairs were rough under his head, though he could scarcely feel them through the callouses on his palm and fingers.

"Feedin' them three mules goin' to be too much," Bully said, figuring to himself on how much grass there was in the pasture and how much feed there was in the barn and on how much a sack of oats cost in town. "If they ain't workin', and if we can't get back into that field to make some kind of a crop, it look to me like feedin' all of them mules goin' to be too much."

He could not see how they would be able to get back in there to do anything about a crop. It was nearly the middle of June now, and even if the water did start falling it would be another two weeks before all of it would be drained off, and the bottom land would be left as nothing but a big mud puddle. It would be the end of July before the ground became dry enough to walk on, much less be dry enough to take a plow. On top of that, he had borrowed about the limit the bank would let him have, and the cost for seed to plant again would stop him right there.

It would do no good to plant again. July was too late. February was when you planted cotton if you wanted it to make in time to start picking by the middle of August. And July was a long way from February. You might replant some washed-out cotton in March, and he had done it as late as April, but you couldn't put in a whole crop and expect it to make out the summer and be to the point where it would mature in the heat of August. July was a long way from February, and no cotton crop was going to be made in two months. He might plant some sorghum down there, or some maize, and that might make; but you couldn't tell—it all depended on how the season was, whether the water got off the ground in time, and whether the sun got hotter and hotter through the summer and baked the ground so hard you could throw a brick down on it and the brick would break.

"I don't see, Papa," Cleveland said, turning this time so that he could look at Bully, "I don't see how we goin' to make any more crop here this year."

"We done made our crop," Bully answered him. "We done already made it this year. We made our cotton crop for the river again, and it look to me like this corn is all the crop there's goin' to be unless the water get that too. I don't know about feedin' all three of them mules if we can't work them. Them mules go through this corn in a hurry if the pasture go down this summer."

The pasture was mostly needle grass. The Bermuda was sparse and it would not be enough if the hot weather burnt the grass and dried it up so that it was little more than yellow dust. The mules needed less to eat when they were not working, but they would eat if they could get it. They needed something, and the pasture was not enough. If they ate the corn in the summer, then what were they going to do in the winter? Bully figured on it, and he could not see the end of it.

The bank had carried him about as far as it was going to. It was too much to expect the bank to let him have more money when his crop was gone and there would be no way for him to make a payment in the fall. They might renew the note; he still had the land and the gear to work it, but to renew the note would cost him again. He would have to add the interest to carry the note another year, and still be without any money to start making a crop. The bank might renew and carry him on as he was, but it could not do much to get him back to where he had been.

The match stem was back at Bully's teeth. He scrubbed at them and then sucked on the hollow tooth back in his jaw to get the last of his breakfast out of it. He had left the table and walked through the barn lot and down across the pasture to the cornfield, and down the turnrow to the edge of water to see whether or not it was still rising. The sun had been up while the family ate, and it was higher now, and hot, but Daly and Unca Dempse and the children stayed around the house and the yard, because there was no work they could do in the field while the water stood between the rows. It did not look like there would be any work for them to do for the rest of the summer unless he decided to go in there and cut that corn and haul it out.

Cleveland had followed him about a quarter of an hour later. The boy had been restless. He could not lie around the house and do nothing. He could not just sit on the porch like Unca Dempse and wait for a car or a wagon to go by and hold his attention for the moment of its passing; he could not work like Tina and Daly did at cleaning the house and feeding and watering the chickens in the lot; he could not spend his time sleeping as did Vincent; and he could not play in the yard like Hoodoo and Little Suster, building graveyards, digging ditches, drawing little square fields, planting grass for cotton rows, and pouring a bucket of water over the field for a flood. Cleveland was restless with no work to do, and he would walk the road, or catch a ride in to town and stay in town on Saturday and come dragging back to the place about the middle of Monday afternoon.

Bully had no blame for him. Bully was restless also, restless with watching the water stand on the field and with wondering what had happened to the black-faced cow and with figuring on what he was going to do next. He hated to think about it, but he figured that maybe he and Cleveland could go in to town and get some work, or if they went up and saw John Chaney when the white man was out there to look at his place that lay just up the river from them, they might be able to get some day labor from him. All of the white man's land was not under water. Most of that pasture he had along the Navasot' was, since it joined Bully's place on the river and lay no higher. But across the road he had hill land where he had moved his cattle when the water started coming up. And out toward the Brazos he had land that still was above the flood. Water stood in some of the low fields, but if it drained off in time he would still make a crop. There were only the crops out there in the wide flatlands below his headquarters that were drowned out, and the people in his houses there had to sit and hope the water would not come any higher up the porch steps. Thinking about all of the white man's drowned crops was hard for Bully to do; there was enough of John Chaney's land under water to make Bully's place look by comparison about as big as a lone seed tick on the side of a Brahman bull, but still the white man had cotton that was not touched by the river, and still he would gather a crop in the fall, and they might get some day labor there if he could use them during the summer.

"Papa," Cleveland asked, turning at last from his position against the fence, "you thinkin' about sellin' a couple of them mules if you don't find no way to use them?" He stretched his arms out to ease the muscles and rubbed with his hands where the wire barbs had pressed into the skin of his forearms.

Bully shifted himself, changing feet, lifting his left foot to rest on the lowest strand of the fence. "I guess so," he reflected. "I reckon that's goin' to be the thing to do. We can't figure on makin' no crop here this year, and I don't see how we goin' to carry three mules through the winter." He shook his head. "I don't see how we goin' to carry none of us through the winter, much less three mules. But who goin' to buy them? Nobody want them mules—they too old. And nobody goin' to pay me anything for that team. I wouldn't even try to sell that Beck mule; she do well to bring five dollars from a glue factory."

Bully looked around toward Cleveland with his forehead wrinkled and his eyes squinting. He did not like to worry in front of Daly and the children, and he would rather not say anything in front of Unca Dempse, because that would get the old man started and he would go on for an hour or more, punching at the floor with his stick and sitting there fuming and talking and not doing a bit of good. But Cleveland was grown; the boy did as much work on the place as Bully. Bully could talk to him about how things stood. Cleveland might like to stay late in town on Saturday night, and he might like to get a little drunk every now and then and hang around with the women and spend money on that Ruby Lee girl who was Book Turner's daughter, but still the boy was grown, and he was smart, and he would have known how things stood anyhow.

Bully depended on Cleveland when it came to the making of a crop. Vincent was old enough to be of use, but he hardly did more work than Hoodoo. Bully was uncertain whether Vincent was sickly and truly had no more strength than his younger brother, or whether he was putting on. In either case, there was no counting on the boy for help. Cleveland was the mainstay; between them they could make out, and Bully could talk with Cleveland about selling the mules. He had to talk with somebody.

"I reckon we better try to sell the team," Bully said. "They eat more corn than they worth anyhow, and that Beck mule be enough for us to get the corn in with and to work in Daly's garden. We better let them go till it look like we can make a crop again, and then I can find us a team somewhere. But I don't know who goin' to buy them; I don't know who goin' to pay money for them mules."

"How much you want for them, Papa?" Cleveland asked. "How much you reckon they worth?"

Bully turned around to look across the pasture toward the mules. The Beck mule was off by herself, close to the fence in the far corner, with her head down so she could pull at the taller grass that grew along the fence row. The Pete mule and the blue mule were not eating. They stood neck against neck, facing each other under the little elm tree that stood out there in the middle of the pasture, and they bit at each other's shoulders, scratching with their teeth where the flies had been. While Bully and Cleveland watched, the blue mule clamped his teeth together too hard and pinched the Pete mule's skin, and the Pete mule squealed and backed his ears and swung his head around to bite higher up on the blue mule's neck. But that was all there was to it; neither one of them had the energy to whirl around and start kicking. They separated and moved out from the tree and began lipping the scant Bermuda grass that grew in between the needle-grass shoots.

"I don't know," Bully said, rubbing his hand over his face and chin again. "They might bring twenty, twenty-five dollars. I reckon if we could get fifty dollars for that team we ought to let them go." Then he stopped and thought. "But they backin' my note at the bank. I can't sell them mules unless the bank say I can. Lawd, I nearly forgot about that."

"I buy the mules, Papa," Cleveland said. "I give you forty dollars for the mules."

"You do what?" Bully's eyes were squinted again, and he jerked his head around to look at Cleveland, his face frowning with surprise. "What you mean, you buy the mules?"

Cleveland straightened himself and looked at Bully. "I say I buy the mules from you for forty dollars if you let me pay you off best I can. The bank don't need to know. If they ask you can say you lend the mules to me."

"What you tryin' to do, boy?" Bully growled. "What good it goin' to do for you to buy the mules if we tryin' to get them off the place? You don't need to stand there and fun with me about buyin' the mules."

"I take them off the place," Cleveland said. "I take them with me when I go if you want me to, or you can keep them till I pay you out. But I want them mules, Papa—I'm goin' to need them mules."

"Howcome?" Bully asked. "Howcome you goin' to need the mules? We ain't goin' to make no crop here."

"I know that," Cleveland said. "That's why I been out to see

Mr. John Chaney and ask him could I go to work for him. It don't look to me like I can do anything here; it look to me like I ought to get out from here if I'm goin' to, and I ask the white man in town could he use me. He say he give me day labor this summer, choppin' cotton, and in the fall I'm goin' to try to get me a place to make a crop for him if I can get the mules to do it with. Sell me the mules, Papa." Cleveland stopped talking suddenly. His face was blank as he looked at his father, but his eagerness showed in the way his body leaned forward slightly. It would be hard to say when he previously had talked that much at one time.

"Lawd God," Bully said, realizing for sure that Cleveland was grown and that the boy was old enough to make up his own mind and plan for himself. "How you goin' to make a crop?" he asked. "You can't take no place and make a crop by yo'self."

"I ain't goin' to try to make a crop by myself," Cleveland answered. "Ruby Lee goin' to help me. We goin' to get married next week and move to a house on Mr. John's place and do day labor for him. She help me make the crop if I get those mules."

"Lawd God," Bully said again. "You ain't said a word to me —you ain't told Daly nothin'. When you-all decide you was goin' to get married?"

"Last Sadday. I found out that Mr. John let us move out there and give us work. We couldn't come out here. The house too crowded now. And they nothin' for me to do here; it look like I ought to go."

"But howcome you didn't say nothin'? Howcome you didn't tell me or yo' mama?"

Cleveland ducked his head and turned back toward the fence. Bully was not surprised that he had said nothing; the boy was closemouthed and always had been, but it looked like he could have told them.

"I told you now," Cleveland said. "We goin' to get married

in town next Sunday." He shoved his hands into his pockets. "It ought not to be nothin' new to you. I been goin' to see her a long time."

"Lawd God," Bully said.

Cleveland was right. It was nothing new. The boy was grown; they had to expect it to come sometime. And yet Bully could not be too glad about it, though it was hard for him to realize clearly why it was that he hated to think about Cleveland's leaving, and had hated to think about it for so long that he had come to take it for granted that the boy would stay on there with them, staying with the place, and that if he got married he would bring his wife out there. He was part of the family, and with him the family was strong, maybe even strong enough to fight the river and the floodwater. Without him, Bully didn't know. But he could not expect Cleveland to stay; there was nothing there to keep him. The floodwaters would not keep Cleveland, the drowned crops would not, and the prospect of a year with no crop would not.

Bully opened the gap and stepped through. The sun was rising higher, and they ought to be getting back to the house to break up stovewood if Daly were going to fix dinner. "Let's go down and look at the water again before we go to the house," Bully said. "I want to see if it's started to fall."

Cleveland stepped through the gap and closed it behind him. He walked beside Bully, and they went down the turnrow toward the edge of the water. They had passed halfway the width of the cornfield before Bully spoke again.

"You pay me when you can," he said, looking at the ground ahead of him as he walked. "We won't say nothin' about it, and I let you have the mules."

CHAPTER ELEVEN

The cushion of John Chaney's green pickup had a permanent dent in it where the big man sat. The springs of the driver's seat sagged, and the imitation leather upholstery was wrinkled, beginning to crack. The back rest had a hollow in it, and a stained spot where sweat from John Chaney's back had darkened the covering. The green Studebaker pickup was new; it had no dents in the fenders, nor were there any rattles. The truck bed itself had lost very little of its factory paint. But the miles were piling up on the speedometer, and the seat under the wheel where John Chaney sat was sagging, because the white man mortally drove that truck.

He could run the wheels off one in a year and still not haul much in it beside himself, and he had needed that Studebaker by the time the dealer got it in. The hood was green, and the doors and the top of the cab were green, but no one looking at the back end of the truck could have told its color, because the red dust of the river bottoms had settled there so thick that all the paint was covered. John Chaney had no time to leave that truck anywhere to have it washed, and he was not likely to pull it up in front of his house in town and use the lawn hose while he washed it himself. The dust could settle on the truck and stay there until a rain washed it off or else balled it up into clinging mud which held onto the body and was later covered by still more dust; because that truck was going to be on the road every day, making a run to the bottoms, rolling down the narrow turnrows, cutting along the big road to the headquarters, even straddling a row of cotton and taking off across a field if the white man could see no other way to get to where he wanted to go.

On the highway going back into town, when John Chaney hit the pavement and eased her up a couple of notches more, a little bit of the red dust might blow off, a few grains of it that had not anchored themselves well; and when he went up to his blackland farm, or to the sandy land, or the grasslands along the Navasot', he would hit the gray dust and the white dust that rose off the rocktopped roads; but the red clung and predominated, because it was out there along the Brazos, where those wide fields and flat acres of red earth yielded a fast crop and a big one, that John Chaney spent most of his time.

He came near to living in that truck when the crop was making. He carried his lunch in there with him, because he was a big man and he had to have his dinner no matter what he was doing or where that pickup had carried him by noontime.

John Chaney carried a Thermos jug of water beside him on the cushion of the pickup. He had plenty of room for it there, and for his lunch too, because it was seldom that he had another man riding with him in the cab. He might bring the county agent out to the bottoms to look over the crops, or he might take a friend out from town to look at one of his best steers or a fine white-faced bull, but ordinarily John Chaney rode alone and carried his lunch with him on the seat, and his water jug, because he was a big man, and a sweating man, and a thirsty one.

He wore khaki most of the time, or else he would have on a white shirt and a pair of tight khaki pants, but the morning would not be half over before the back of the shirt would be wringing wet, and dark patches under his armpits would be growing downward along his sides, and the waist of the pants, stretched tight, would soak through.

His face stayed red, so red that some people said he could get his complexion only by spending half his time with a whisky jug; but it was sunshine and not alcohol that made his face glow with a redness that nearly matched that of the water of the Brazos River. John Chaney was a light-skinned man, and his hair was fair. When it grayed there would not be much change, since he had been cotton-topped from a boy on. He wore a broad-brimmed hat, a cattleman's straw with a pinched crown and punched air holes; but even the shade of the wide straw was not enough to keep the sun off his face all day, and it did nothing to keep the dry and burning winds that blew across the fields from touching his skin and leaving it fiery. He didn't blister and he didn't peel, but every year, from late spring until winter, he had a face that was as red as the tail-light on the pickup.

He wore cowboy boots on his feet. The legs of his pants hung over the outside of the boots and covered the inlay and the stitching in the tops, but he always drove with those boots on, and that cattleman's hat, as if the farming were only a side line with him and his main interest lay back with the white-faces that had brought him his first money. The way it was now, he spent about nine-tenths of his time with the crops and one-tenth of it with the livestock. There was no time left over for him to spend in town with his wife.

Not that it mattered; it had been years since they went any-where together. Chaney saw her when he came home at night, that was about all. If he was gone from the house all day there was nothing unusual in it. She had her meetings, and her bridge club, and her trips out of town. And who could say what there was between them when Chaney came home at night? Once they were both behind the doors of the house they were beyond range of the town's tongue, and there was no talk of John Chaney and his wife. Chaney was a busy man; his wife was a busy woman.

John Chaney was going to keep moving; nobody was going to lay off while his cotton was in the grass. His big trucks would be in town long before sunup, making the rounds to pick up the extra choppers from their houses in Freedmantown. The trucks would burn the road coming out that six miles of paved highway before turning off to go up the packed dirt of the road that ran alongside the big Brazos for a while, then cut between the fields toward the barns and the store and the houses of John Chaney's headquarters. In the afternoon it would be sundown before the flat-bedded trucks started loading up again with people, and it would be dark before they finished delivering the town hands back to their houses in Freedmantown.

In between the run of the trucks, the hands would be strung out across the fields, their hoes sharp, with the blades cleaned to shining by the abrasion of the red earth. The rise and fall of the hoes would send flashes of reflected sunlight to blink in the air and sparkle and be seen from the distant highway to mark the field where the choppers were trying to catch up with the cultivator gangs, trying to get the cotton clean before the rains got to it.

And John Chaney drove that pickup. He was not easy on it; he never took time to be easy when it was all he could do in a single day to get out there to the bottoms to see that his choppers were lined out in the field, and that the plow hands hooked their teams to the cultivators and got in there to killing that grass without losing time on the turnrows, and to see that the two tractors were running in the longer fields that lay up the river on the far side of the headquarters. The white man did not have time to fool around and pet the Studebaker if he was to see that his work was going right in the red flatlands and still be able to leave the bottoms and get back to town and on the other side of town and out to the blackland and the pasture along the Navasot' to see after his cattle. He got around; he covered the country in a day, because John Chaney liked to look at his land and his crops. He liked to look at his cattle, and since it was cattle that had made him his first money and let him buy the land that he needed for big farming, he babied those whitefaces and kept them on good mesquite grass, and he raised feed for them so that he would be able to carry them through the winter if they failed to bring him the price he wanted in the fall.

Before he had spread his holdings and managed to take in so much of the Brazos bottom land, John Chaney had ridden his horse to the field, and he would sit there on the turnrow to watch how the choppers walked through the cotton. But the horse came to be too slow; there were too many fields to cover, and the horse was unable to get Chaney from one place to another quickly enough. That was one reason John Chaney bought a pickup, and got in the habit of buying one, and kept on buying a new pickup every year or year and a half after that. The other reason had to do with why his voice was so high and sharp, so shrill to be the voice of a big man.

John Chaney should have had a deep voice to go with his frame. His neck was thick, and now that he was growing fat it was even thicker. He had broad shoulders and a wide back, and since he quit riding the horse his waist was widening and thickening to catch up with the back and shoulders. Light blue eyes, quick and nervous, were deep-sunk on either side of a nose that started out straight and low but ended up with wide, flared nostrils and a slightly flattened tip. The shape of his nose might have had something to do with the nasal quality of his voice, but it was the scar on his throat, down near the jointure of his neck and shoulders, that had most to do with making it high and shrill.

He might have had a deeper voice and might still have been riding his white horse and been wearing spurs on the heels of his boots, if Forty Davis had not waited in the bushes along the bank of the creek and cut loose with both barrels of a shotgun as the white man rode by.

Forty had been a small man, with a skin as black as Cul Sally's, but he was quick and he was smart, and he was the lead hand in John Chaney's chopping gang the summer that he took his shotgun from behind the door and loaded it and slipped down there to the creek to lie in the bushes and wait. Forty owed the white man a bond and had been working for him out there in the bottoms ever since John Chaney got him out of jail on a cattle-stealing charge; but that was not the reason that Forty lay in the bushes and cut loose with both barrels of the shotgun.

It never did come out exactly what the reason was, since Forty did not come to trial for the shooting. Forty had never before had any trouble with the white man. The cow-stealing was his one big error. John Chaney had shouted at Forty in the field and raised hell with him, but that was nothing new. The white man raised hell with all his hands when the crop was making. The only reason the sheriff could give was that Forty must just have gone crazy like niggers will do.

That might have been true; Forty was bound to have been crazy or nervous, one or the other, for not waiting until John Chaney got close enough. After all the planning he had done, and after all the lying out there in the bushes waiting for the white man to ride by, Forty cut loose too soon, and he pulled both triggers at the same time, and all of those lead pellets went wide of the white man, so far over the top of his head that he never heard the wind of them. But the horse heard the blast from the gun muzzle and, since he was a fractious horse anyhow, not used to having things boom out from the bushes thirty yards in front of him, he jumped sideways so fast that he just left John Chaney there in the air without a saddle under him.

And the white man turned over in the air, surprised and tumbling as he was, and fell flat face down in the bushes and bloodweeds there at the edge of the turnrow. A dead bloodweed stalk, broken off halfway down and standing there hard and sharp as a lance, caught John Chaney in the throat, just below the Adam's apple, and that was why his voice was so high and shrill, and that was why he could not control it sometimes when it broke and left him whispering.

He came near to bleeding to death before anybody could get to him from the fields and carry him in to town, and it left him so weak that when he was up and about again and ready to come out to the bottoms he started riding in a pickup truck.

Forty had not touched the white man with those two charges of number six shot, but he still managed to do plenty of damage. He must have been a little crazy, else he would never have tried to come back to his house after the sheriff had the dogs out there in the bottoms after him. The dogs trailed him there, and Forty's wife stood back while the sheriff and about five of the men who had been made deputies for the hunt searched the house. The sheriff didn't find anything, but the men outside and the dogs did. The dogs kept whining and snuffling under the house, lunging against the ends of their leashes, and when somebody finally got around to shining a light under the house, there was Forty treed like a coon in a hollow log.

They asked him to come out, but Forty wouldn't move, and nobody would go under there after him. The sheriff tried to reason with Forty, but that didn't do any good either. Forty wouldn't come out. So the sheriff had to shoot him, aiming down the beam of light from a flashlight that a deputy held, with Forty's wife sitting above in the house, hollering.

She was a pretty, light-skinned woman, and Forty was all she had, since she was expecting a baby and couldn't work. But John Chaney took care of her. He gave her enough money to go off to an aunt that she had living in Fort Worth, and the money was enough to take care of the baby's being born. She had been a mighty pretty woman for a man like Forty to marry, she was so light, so coffee-colored, and had such a nice-looking face and shape on her. She never did say anything about any reason that Forty might have had for shooting at the white man, and then John Chaney gave her the money and she was gone, and the only way anybody could figure it out was that Forty, just as the sheriff said, had gone a little crazy like a nigger will do. John Chaney had not worn out three pickups before the whole thing was talked out and forgot about.

But there were plenty of changes in it for John Chaney. Forty had not come close to him with that squirrel shot, but the bloodweed had caught him, and when he was well again his voice was different. For some reason his wife moved into a separate room and started sleeping by herself, and she started taking more week-long trips out of town to visit her relatives in Houston. Chaney bought her a car, and she took it and drove it, but nobody ever saw Chaney riding in there with her. They didn't go anywhere together. And Chaney quit riding the white horse, because the pickup made it easier for him to get about over the bottoms to look at his crops, and his crops were getting bigger and needed more looking after. He bought land along the Brazos, he picked up some farms back in the sandy-land hills and threw them together and started farming them with tractors and raising watermelons on them, and he bought more pasture land along the Navasot' and started running more whitefaces on it. He was kept busy.

He needed that green Studebaker to get around in. He had too much territory to cover; he had to move fast to keep his work moving fast, and a horse would never do it. He stayed home little and seldom saw his wife except for the short time they were together at supper after he came home late in the evening. He took his lunch and his Thermos jug of water and left early in the morning, and the lunch and the water rode beside him on the seat of the green pickup while he burned the road out to the Navasot', to the blackland and the hill farms, and out the paved highway to the bottoms where the river cut through the red flatland and where the green pickup was like a shuttle moving through the network of roads and turnrows, with the dust kicked up by the tires and the truck's passing mounting into the air as a cloud and then settling to make a blanket of red over the green, broad leaves of the cotton. And the dust which settled on the bed and body of the truck covered its green to make it as red as the cotton leaves and as red as the water in the wide river that curved slowly through the cradled land.

CHAPTER TWELVE

Cleveland had gone from the farm on the Navasot', and summer with him. The fall followed after, and now it was winter as Bully walked across the pasture toward the persimmon tree at the lower end, with Hoodoo running along in front of him.

"I was comin' back to the house when I seen old Beck kickin' with her feets," Hoodoo said. "She down in the gully gruntin' and can't get up."

Bully shielded his eyes from the morning sun and tried to see across the pasture to the spot where the mule lay almost hidden by the grass. Both legs of his overalls were wet to the knees from the dew that was not yet dried. "Maybe she just down wallerin'," Bully said. "I'm sho' goin' to whip you, boy, if you lyin' just to get me to walk down in the pastuh."

"She ain't wallerin', Papa," Hoodoo said. "Old Beck down."

Bully spit through his teeth and rolled his chew of tobacco to the other side of his jaw. His arms swung at his sides, and his faded blue jumper hung loose on his shoulders. The mud balled up on his shoes and he kicked his feet to sling off heavy gobs of it while he walked across the needle-grass pasture after Hoodoo. "Ain't no mule goin' to waller in a gully," Bully said.

Hoodoo ran ahead. "Yonder old Beck is," he shouted, pointing to prove that he was not lying. "She ain't dead yet, but she might as well be."

The mule lay grunting on her side. She had pawed up the wet dirt on the sides of the slight dip in the ground in which she lay, and her thrashing legs had rubbed the needle grass until it was bent slick and smooth. She lay with her head stretched out and her sides heaving while the breath sucked in and out through her nostrils, flattening them and spreading them. She opened her eyes and nickered when Bully and Hoodoo walked up to her.

They stopped and looked down at her. "We got to try to

get her up," Bully said. "She might live if us can get her on her feet."

The mule grunted and lifted her head and then rolled, trying to get her feet under her; but the weight of her body was down in the gully, and she was unable to roll over to the level ground.

Bully moved back while the wildly pawing feet dug at the earth and flung clods of mud and matted grass backward. "She too weak," he said. "She must have been there all night." He walked around her and felt of the mud she had plastered on her underside in her rollings.

With his hand Hoodoo scraped at the dried persimmon caked around his mouth. "I never seen her till I like to run up on her," he said. "I was comin' back from the persimmon tree and she was layin' there in the gully gruntin' with her belly up in the air."

"We'll have to leave her there," Bully said. "Us can't lift her up. If us get a bucket of oats and bring them down here and let her eat she might be able to roll over out of the gully."

They looked at her a minute longer and then turned to go back to the barn.

The mule lay still after they had gone, tired from her struggles. She was long and gaunt, and her hipbones were like knobs that were almost bursting through the skin. Her red hair was scarce, even in its winter coat. From the under side of her neck all the hair had rubbed off against the ground. She lay in the little depression that was the rain-washed head of a gully meandering down through Bully's place toward the creek that bounded it on the south. The mule's sides heaved as she breathed. One nostril was almost plugged with mud. Her breaths were long and slow, widely spaced, as she lay with her neck stretched and her head extended on the cold, wet earth.

The wind that came from the north bent the sparse brown needle grass of the pasture and ruffled the few longer hairs of the mule's coat and lifted the uncaked hair of her mane. The

January wind was cold and damp. It held the promise of more rain as it blew across the fields that were brown with frostbitten Johnson grass and dry, broken cornstalks. In the bottoms the cotton rows were hidden under matted, flood-drifted grass, and doves and killdees and field larks that walked the turnrows in search of seeds from the grass clogged their toes with clinging balls of the black mud and left strange, misshapen tracks on the water-leveled land.

Hoodoo walked around the yard to the front of the house while Bully went into the barn to empty the last of a sack of oats into the feed bucket. The mud that covered Hoodoo's shoes was cold; it chilled his feet inside the leather. The left leg of his overalls had a tear at the knee, and orange of a mashed persimmon showed against the black of his skin.

He pushed open the door and walked into the room at the front of the house, where Unca Dempse sat in his rawhide-bottomed chair close to the coals that glowed in the fireplace. The scalloped edges of the smoke-yellowed newspapers that covered the mantel rustled when Hoodoo opened the door. With his walking stick the old man was poking at a log to try to make it stay on top of the pile of coals.

"Old Beck down, Unca Dempse," Hoodoo said. "Old Beck down on the ground and can't get up."

"What you say, Hoodoo?" Unca Dempse asked, hunched over in his chair while he sucked on the cane stem of his pipe.

"The mule down," Hoodoo said. "Old Beck down in a gully."

Unca Dempse took his pipe from between his gums and spit into the ashes. He moved around in his chair, turning his head so that he could look at Hoodoo. "I done said that mule was goin' to die," he grunted. He wiped the bony back of his hand across his lips and rubbed at his chin. "I done said that mule was goin' to die." His voice rose to a quaver. "Hoodoo, I done told yo' papa to give that mule corn."

Daly came from the kitchen with the coffeepot in her hand.

She stood in the doorway with the sleeves of her dress rolled up over her strong brown arms. Her hair was done up in a knot at the back of her head and had a stocking cap on it. There was a dip of snuff in her lower lip and a snuff brush in her mouth. "Hoodoo, quit pickin' at Unca Dempse," she said. "You chillun worry him with yo' hollerin' around."

"The mule down, Mama," Hoodoo said. "Old Beck down in the field and can't get up."

Daly slapped at Little Suster, who was trying to push past her out of the kitchen into the room where Hoodoo and Unca Dempse were. "Don't tell me," she said. "I can't do nothin'. Get out of here and don't come botherin' me. I'm got to fix you-all some dinner."

Hoodoo backed out of the room into the cold air outside, and then ran around the house to catch up with his father. Bully was carrying the oats and a bucket of water down the trail behind the garden fence and across the pasture, where the earlier trip had left the needle grass bent in a path to old Beck.

They found her lying in the gully just as she was when they left her. The black scars of dirt showed through the torn needle grass where she had pawed. Her head was stretched out, but her nostrils were flared and still, and the swollen sides were not moving.

Bully put his buckets on the ground and looked at the mule while he dug in his jumper pocket for his tobacco, his hand wandering there of its own accord while he looked down at the mule. Hoodoo squatted on the ground close to the mule's head, and then he turned around to look up at Bully.

"Papa," he said, "old Beck done dead."

They sat around the table in the kitchen while Daly carried corn bread and winter turnips from the stove.

Bully sat at one end of the table and Unca Dempse sat at the other. Hoodoo and Little Suster sat with their backs against the wall on one side, and Vincent came out of the side room to sit across from them, next to Tina. Even at midday the room was full of dark corners. Daly kept the outside door closed in the winter, and the only light for the room came in the window cut in the west wall. The wooden, hinged door to it was opened against the side of the house, but the clouded sky let only a dim light into the room, and the opened window made the whole house cold and drafty. The wood stove took up a whole end of the kitchen, and Daly's paper-lined shelves for dishes were ranged against one wall. The table holding her dishpan stood under the window, and the rest of the room was taken up at mealtime by the family.

There was a big pot of greens and turnips that had been cooked down until the juice was rich. A piece of fat bacon had been cooked with them, and Bully divided it carefully.

"I want me some fresh sausage," Vincent said. "I ain't never had enough fresh meat. You-all grab the meat away from me till I don't get nothin' but a little old slice of ham or a piece of chitlins. I could eat a whole yard of chitlins now." Vincent did not weigh much more than Hoodoo. The black skin of his arms was dry and crusty, and the thinness of his fingers made them look like claws while he clutched a piece of corn bread and mopped it in the juice that was on his plate.

"If I could have bought some shoats in the summer we would have had plenty of meat," Bully said. "We would have had meat enough to last us all the winter, and maybe in the spring we would still have been eatin' off of the sides of bacon."

"The shoats would die," Daly said tonelessly. She went to her seat by the stove and took her plate on her lap. She looked toward the table where Bully sat softening his corn bread in the juice from the greens and drinking from the tin cup of coffee by his plate. "Dead mules and hogs, and drownded cotton and nubbin corn is all the place is good for." She chopped the words out while her eyes blazed at Bully as if she were blaming him for the whole trouble.

Unca Dempse looked up from his plate. He raised a hand to

wipe at his lips and then said, "I done told you that mule goin' to die without no corn to eat."

"Lawd, Unca Dempse," Bully said, "I know the mule need corn, but I ain't had none for her. She done cleaned up all them nubbins but a few for the chickens, and I ain't had no feed of no kind for that mule except that last bucket of oats I was goin' to try to get her to eat. When corn bring a dollar and a half in town I got to take it in and sell it. These chillun got to have somethin' to eat too. Us had to make out to get through the fall."

"I done told you that mule goin' to die," Unca Dempse said.

Hoodoo got up from the table and rolled on the floor and kicked and grunted. "She was layin' there in the gully with her feets tearin' up the ground," he said while Vincent and Tina and Little Suster looked at him. "I walked right up on her and she couldn't get up."

After dinner Bully went out to stand on the front porch. The air was still cold, but the position of the sun was indicated by a bright spot in the clouds. The road running in front of the house was deserted, and even the ruts were old and had clear water standing in them.

Hoodoo came out of the house to stand beside his father and look up at him. The boy was quiet for once, serious-faced while he looked at his father staring out over the empty road.

"If the mule had lived," Bully said slowly, looking back over his plan as he spoke, "us could have got the ground for a garden broke up. And the cornfield be dry enough to plow in a couple of days it it don't rain again. Lawd knows we ought to get some sort of a place busted up if us aim to make a crop this year."

"Cleveland got a team," Vincent said from the door behind Bully. "Howcome Cleveland couldn't bring that blue mule and Pete mule out here to break up the land?"

"I might see," Bully said without turning to look at Vincent. "I might see. But he goin' to need them mules in the spring. He might come out here and bust up the ground, but us can't make no crop unless we got some way to work it."

"Cleveland taken the team," Vincent said. "If he hadn't carried the mules with him we could have got the land broke up."

Bully turned then. "Don't talk back to me, boy. Cleveland needed the mules. Us couldn't make no crop here after the water come, and he taken the mules to get him a job. Don't fault him none—not when he paid money for them mules and helped us through the fall like he done."

Vincent shook his head stubbornly. "Cleveland taken the good mules," he said. "He left us that no 'count one."

"Cleveland need that team," Bully told him. "If he goin' to farm for Mr. John he got to have that team, and us couldn't make no crop here when he left."

"Us can't make no crop now," Vincent said, "without no mule."

Unca Dempse came out of the house to stand in the back yard and watch Bully cut wood for Hoodoo to carry into the kitchen. The sun was going down behind the clouds that had covered it all day. The north wind had quieted and the air was still. The smoke rose straight up out of the chimney in a thin blue streak, and down toward the trees that bordered the creek it was already dark and cold where backwater from the river was lapping at the full banks. Frogs along the creek and in the ditches at the side of the road filled the evening with their croaking.

"You better get plenty of wood cut up and in the house," Unca Dempse said. "It's goin' to get cold, and I don't want the fire to go out in the middle of the night and leave me to freeze to death. It's goin' to blow up a fresh norther durin' the night."

He sucked on his pipe and punched at the ground with his stick while he thought of his bed at night when the fire died down in the fireplace in the front room, and how between the covers he would be drawn up and shivering except for Hoodoo and Little Suster sleeping on either side of him. He could feel their warm bodies against him in the night and he was glad they were there.

The massed noise of the frogs rose in almost deafening waves, but the sound was so rolling and continuous in the still evening air that Bully forgot that he heard it above the rhythmic blows of his ax.

"Lawd God, I wish I knowed where I could get me a mule," he thought while he laid the oak poles across the chopping block and cut them into firewood lengths. But he knew that the lack of a mule was not all of his trouble, and the realization came to him that even if he had a fat pair of the biggest mules on John Chaney's Brazos Bottom farm he would not be able to break the grip that was on him. The land along the creek and the river was rich. The soil was thick and fertile, and the crops grew tall and sucked up the water and nourishment for dark green leaves; but if one short, washing flood swept down the creek in summer or backed up from the river in the spring, he was done.

He needed to work his place like the white man did his far-stretching fields along the big Brazos, fifteen miles away. He needed seeds to plant and tools to work the crops when the grass got high. He needed money to play against the river so he could plant early and beat the dry weather in June and July. If he had these, and a flood drowned the crop, then he could buy again and plant again, playing his hand against the river's until he won out.

"Sho'ly this year I'd make me a crop," Bully figured while he cut the wood and split the kindling for Hoodoo to carry in, "if I could just find me a mule somewhere."

The wind came up about ten o'clock. It blew hard for a while and then rain started and fell steadily. Bully heard the rain falling on the roof while he lay in bed beside Daly. He got up and put pans under the leaks in the kitchen. He came back to stand by the fire and stir it up and put on another stick of wood. The flames flickered in the drafts that came in through the cracks in the chimney and up between the planks of the floor. Bully went back to bed and lay there with his eyes open while he listened to the rain falling and the water dripping into the pans on the kitchen floor. He heard Unca Dempse snoring while he slept in his bed, warm with Little Suster and Hoodoo on either side of him.

CHAPTER THIRTEEN

"You never complained before about this place," John Chaney said, looking past Joe Coby to the fields that came up close to the house. "You've been here a long time, Joe; I thought you were satisfied with the place. You've been making a good crop here just about every year, and I figured you were the man that knew how to work it for me."

The green pickup truck stood at the edge of the road in front of Joe Coby's house. The white man sat inside the cab with one hand still on the steering wheel, but his body was canted to the right and his head was lowered to let him see out of the window. Joe Coby had one foot on the running board and his hat was in his hand. He was twisting the hat around and around, rotating it between his hands as he leaned forward with his right elbow propped against the door of the truck. A quick, head-ducking smile came and went on his smooth face, because Joe was a little nervous standing like this after stopping the boss man and asking what the chances were of his moving.

"I ain't complainin', Mr. John. I don't mean it to sound like that. I just thought I'd ask about us gettin' out of here and see couldn't we find a better house."

"Anything wrong with that house there? Looks to me like it's standin' up straight as any house out here."

"Nawsuh, ain't nothin' you'd say wrong with it. The roof leak a little; them boards on the porch floor missin', and some of them a little bit rotten. We thought if you was goin' to have another place we'd like to ask for it first. It look like a change be good; I just like to have a change."

John Chaney cleared his throat, laughing while he was doing it, so that the air got mixed up in his throat and choked him, and he had to cough before he could speak again.

"You're so God-damned lazy, Joe," he said, "you're so God-damned lazy and finicky that you won't fix this place. If you stayed home on Saturday evening instead of goin' to town you could have this house tighter than anything this side of that seed barn up there by the store. What you're wantin' to do is move into a place that somebody else has fixed up for you."

"Nawsuh, Mr. John. It just look like we been here so long. We thought maybe we could work better and make us a better crop if we got on another place." Joe had his hat going around now, and his head was turned with the profile to the white man. Joe was looking down at the ground as he talked. He was wishing he had told Lula to keep her mouth shut when she told him to come out and stop the white man. He had figured the white man wouldn't like for him to be asking about moving. He knew John Chaney; that man could ride a tenant if he took a notion to. Joe wished he hadn't let Lula talk him into coming out here.

Joe and his wife had had an early dinner. Lula took her time, but started fixing the meal not long after they brought their hoes from the field. They were sitting down to the table before twelve o'clock.

"Mr. John goin' to be headin' back this way before long," Lula said. "Why don't you watch out for him on the road and see won't he stop when he come by?"

"Howcome?" Joe Coby asked, more interested in his dinner and in the idea of having half a day off than in watching for John Chaney's pickup to come down the turnrow road. "He come by here every day about this time. Howcome you want me to stop him now? You want to ask him for a ride to town?"

"Joe, you needn't be a fool," his wife said. "I don't know where yo' mind is today. All you done all mornin' is worry about that dog, and there ain't nothin' wrong with the dog that he won't get over by tonight."

Lula put her knife and fork on the table and leaned forward so that the motion would make Joe leave off looking at his plate and raise his head to pay attention to what she said. "Howcome you went out of the way to go down there and talk to Clevelan'? Howcome you been tryin' to find out what he aimin' to do? Now is the time to see the white man about gettin' onto that place Clevelan' got, because you know Mr. John ain't goin' to keep that nigger here after the way him and Buddy Boy fought this mornin'."

"I don't know," Joe Coby said, still chewing. "Mr. John didn't say much to Clevelan' about this fight. Clevelan' said the white man didn't tell him nothin'."

"You still a fool, Joe," his wife said. "I told you this mornin' you wouldn't get nothin' out of Clevelan'. That boy don't like you—he don't like nobody—and he keep his mouth so close he ain't goin' to talk to you." Lula saw Joe raise his head and swallow to get his mouth cleared for answering her. The look in his eyes warned her, and she lowered her voice to quit nagging, but her words continued. "You too cautious," she said. "I'd hate to think that because you was too slow to see the white man he went on and gave somebody else that place after he got rid of Clevelan'."

Joe went back to his eating and did not bother to answer her for a while, but when his plate was empty he looked up again and grinned at her. "Ain't nobody ever said he was goin' to get rid of Clevelan'. You know well as I do howcome the man don't want to get rid of that boy long as Ruby Lee down there with him. But if it keep you quiet I'll stop him when he come by and ask him what can he do for me. I been with Mr. John long enough for him to stop and talk to me."

Lula had helped Joe to make up his mind that he was not being treated right, and now Joe was standing at the side of the road with one foot up on the running board of the truck, waiting while the white man sat inside the cab and mopped at his face with a white handkerchief.

John Chaney jammed the handkerchief into his hip pocket. He slid from under the steering wheel and moved to the right side of the cab. Joe moved back as the white man stuck his head out of the window.

"Look yonder, Joe," John Chaney said, making a sweeping motion with his hand to indicate the land that lay along the bank of the creek. "From here clean to the highway and all the way behind us to the headquarters this land is cut up. Your house stands here, and down there is Cul's, and beyond him is Cleveland's. The place is all cut up into little patches of ground. It was that way when I bought it and it's been that way ever since, and now it's losing money for me. You've been with me a long time, Joe, and you know how it is. You-all take the places and farm them for me, but it's all cut up and there are six men doing the work one could do." Joe's hands stopped shifting and the hat was still while he listened to the white man.

John Chaney was wound up. He had to clear his throat to keep on talking, and there was a subdued excitement that showed itself in his voice and in his gestures as he outlined what he was going to do. Joe made a good audience, because his mouth had dropped open a little, and his ears, if they could, would have pricked forward.

"I don't know if I can do it this year," the white man said. "Next year maybe I'll have the tractors, and then if I throw her all together there won't be this little patching of forty acres here and forty acres there with the rows running every which way. There'll be just one big field with the creek on one side and this road on the other. There'll be cotton from here to the highway and clear back to the barns."

"Lawd God," Joe Coby said.

The white man turned toward Joe. "I haven't done that yet," he said. "I'm just thinkin' about doing it. You needn't to worry, Joe. You've been with me a long time—I'll see that you have a place."

"Lawd God," Joe said. "What the others goin' to do?"

"It takes men to run the tractors." John Chaney laughed. "And you know it's goin' to take a lot of choppers to get rid of the grass and a lot of pickers to get the cotton in the wagons. There's goin' to be plenty of work out here, but these houses are liable to go."

Joe was shifting the hat again. The sun was hot to the top of his head, but he did not think about putting on the hat. "I don't reckon it matter, then, Mr. John. I had meant to ask you that if Clevelan' move out, couldn't we get his place?"

Chaney snorted, surprised, as his head darted around. "Who told you Cleveland was goin' to move?" Joe Coby opened his mouth to speak, but Chaney went on: "I hadn't said anything to him yet. I was on my way down there to talk to him when you stopped me."

"Ain't nobody said he goin' to leave. I just thought I ask about the place in case he do move."

"I don't mind tellin' you," John Chaney said, "I have got another place in mind for Cleveland, and I was goin' down there to tell him about it. I'm still workin' on the deal for the place, but I thought I'd let him know about it." Chaney slid under the wheel again. He had to lean his body to the right once more in order to see Joe as he kept on talking. Leaning, he looked past Joe Coby to the yard where the white dog was limping toward the fence, still favoring his right front leg. "What's the matter with the dog?"

"I don't know, Mr. John," Joe answered, turning to suck

through his lips at the dog and call him up closer. "He was like that early this mornin' when I got up. He don't bark at trucks, else I'd say one of the trucks haulin' hands back to town might have hit him in the dark yestiddy evenin'."

John Chaney laughed. "It wasn't me hit that dog," he said. "If he was to get in my way on the road you'd find him still lying there." Chaney wiped his face with the handkerchief again and then bent forward to turn the key in the switch. "If I do move Cleveland out this fall, I reckon you could move down there if you wanted to," he said.

Joe bent to get his hand on the dog's neck as the truck started. "It don't matter," he said. "I just thought I'd ask. But if it just be for a year it don't matter. Whatever you say, Mr. John."

He held the dog while the boss man put the truck in gear and pulled away down the road, the exhaust pipe roaring and dust rising behind the rear wheels. He wished Lula had kept her mouth shut and not made him come out. He had just as soon he didn't know what was on the white man's mind. He had just as soon not think about the one big field running from the headquarters clear to the highways, with tractors in there where his team had been.

Back in the house, Joe did little to satisfy Lula's questioning. She was too eager to suit him, and he did not want to talk. "He say he'd see that we got a place," was all that Joe would mutter for a while. And then he began to add to it. "He say he'd see that we would get a place; he already got one for Clevelan'. He goin' to look out for them. Long as that girl down there he goin' to look out for them."

CHAPTER FOURTEEN

Cleveland was making a turn at the far end of the field, by the creek bank, when the pickup truck roared down the turnrow road from the direction of Joe Coby's house. John Chaney drove fast, as if always he knew where he was going and was in a hurry to get there, and Cleveland saw the dust rising beyond the cornfield as the white man turned toward the cotton lands that lined the creek bank. Cleveland stopped his team in mid-field and heard the sound of the motor coming closer.

"I'm goin' to ask that man again today," he said. "I'm goin' to ask him one more time."

The truck came around the end of the cornfield, bumping. The wheels straddled the narrow turnrow that bordered the field next to the creek bank, and John Chaney drove slowly, with the motor whining in second gear while the pickup rocked over the furrows. There was just barely enough room for the truck to run without mashing down the young cotton. The boss man would have had to drive astraddle a row of cotton to get around the field of corn, and Cleveland pictured to himself how the truck would have turned off the road there by the house and come down through the field, and how Ruby Lee, if she was still at home and had not yet gone to the store, would come to the kitchen door to look out and wonder at John Chaney, thinking, "What's he goin' down there for? Why is he goin' down there to see Clevelan'?" The same question was in Cleveland's mind.

The white man braked to a stop at the end of Cleveland's row. The mules lifted their heads and pricked their ears forward, but Cleveland slapped the lines against their sides and finished the round, bringing the mules to a stop just before they reached the turnrow, with their noses five feet short of touching the front fender of the truck.

"Be God damned," Chaney said. He cursed in the same thin, high voice that made his common run of speech sharp and penetrating. The shrillness of his talk made Cleveland's nerves crawl like a razor would scraping on a pane of glass. "By Christ," Chaney said, opening the door of the truck cab and leaning out to look back at the way he had come. "There's no place to turn around. I'll have to back out all the way to keep from runnin' over that cotton."

Cleveland stood looking at him, still holding to the cultivator handles, wondering what he wanted down here. "Yassuh, sho' will," Cleveland said.

"I hadn't brought the truck down here along this creek for a long time," John Chaney said. "But I wanted to look at this cotton you had behind the cornfield, Cleveland. It's lookin' mighty good and you ought to make a crop this year."

Sitting in the truck, Chaney seemed to be particularly large, because his head nearly touched the roof of the cab when he sat up straight. The heat was not setting well with him. It kept his face red and wet with sweat. The hot July sun kept streams of perspiration trickling down from under the pinch-crowned straw hat and gave the fine red dust something to cling to when it settled. John Chaney kept wiping at his face with his big handkerchief while he sat in the cab of the pickup.

Cleveland waited without saying anything more, standing there behind his cultivator with the rope lines still around his neck. He waited to see if the white man was going to move on in the truck and let him get the team turned around. If all the man came down here to do was look at the crops, then he had seen them, and if he moved, Cleveland could set the cultivator on a new row.

But John Chaney showed no signs of being in a hurry to move. He had killed his motor and was sitting there in the truck as if he meant to stay all afternoon. He finished wiping at his face with the handkerchief and pushed the hat back on his head to let the air cool his forehead. There was a red streak where the sweatband had rested just above his eyebrows. When John Chaney was driving he wore the hat pulled down low in front so that there would be plenty of shade for his eyes. He pushed the hat back and slid out from under the wheel and across the cab to where he could rest an arm in the window on the right side.

"Come here, Cleveland," he said. "God damn, don't stand there in the field all day. I come down here to talk to you."

Cleveland lifted the lines from around his neck and hung them over a cultivator handle. He stepped around the cultivator wheel and walked down the middle beside the Pete mule.

"Yassuh, Mr. John," he said.

Chaney was shaking a cigarette out of the packet he had taken from his shirt pocket, and he put the cigarettes back without offering Cleveland one. "I started to say this to you this morning," John Chaney said, "but I decided I better wait till you cooled off a little. You had Buddy Boy too much on your mind to pay much attention to what I would have had to say."

Cleveland reached for his own tobacco and started dusting the brown flakes from the Bull Durham sack into the rectangle of rice paper. His head was ducked as he grasped one of the drawstrings in his teeth and pulled on the other string with his hand to close the sack, but his eyes were looking upward from under his brows so that he could see the white man. "What is it, Mr. John?" he asked. "I ain't had Buddy Boy on my mind since I left him on the turnrow."

"I may have another place for you in the fall," the white man said. "Your crop here is lookin' good, Cleveland, and it'll look better when you get this field clean, but it seems to me that you'd do better on a different kind of place. You came down here from the Navasot', didn't you?" the white man asked. "You know the country, don't you? You know how to farm that Navasot' land?"

"I knows it pretty well," Cleveland said, wondering if John Chaney didn't remember that he had been raised there, and wondering if he had got hold of some stumpy new ground that needed clearing up. "But I don't know about us movin' up there for you, Mr. John. I been wantin' to talk to you about this crop—"

"You goin' to make a good crop, Cleveland. Looks to me like you goin' to make a bale to the acre, and fifty bushels of corn. But I may need you to get a place in shape for me. I'll get you a pair of mules that will do twice as much work as this bony team you got now. Those mules move too slow. They ain't goin' to be able to get done the work that needs to be done."

Cleveland looked around at Pete and the blue mule. "These mules pretty good, Mr. John. They all right. They don't tromp on no cotton, even if sometime they do be a little slow. I been had these mules ever since I started workin' for you."

"You started last summer," John Chaney remembered. "Those mules were pretty well wore out before you ever got hold of them, Cleveland. Where did you get that team?"

"I bought them from Papa," Cleveland said. "I bought them from him right after I left out yonder and started to choppin' cotton for you."

"Wait a minute," John Chaney said, looking more closely at Cleveland. "You're Bully Webster's boy, ain't you?"

"Yassuh," Cleveland said. "I thought you knew."

John Chaney laughed. He shook his head while he was laughing and took another drag to finish his smoke before flipping the butt away from the truck.

"I swear," he said. "Sometimes I forget. There's so many of you people out here that sometimes I forget who your folks are." He eased himself back under the wheel and leaned forward to turn the key in the switch.

"I'll let you know more about that moving," he said. "I'll get you a better team, Cleveland. It's a wonder them mules don't fall dead in the middle of a row." He started the pickup. "You can get more work done with a better team." He opened the door and leaned out. His head was down on the other side of the truck and Cleveland could not see him, but as the truck started backing down the turnrow Chaney shouted, "You come to see me in town Saturday morning. I ought to know something more then, and I'll want to talk to you some more about moving this fall."

And the motor was whining and growling and the front end bouncing as the wheels climbed over the plowed ground. Beyond the edge of the corn the boss man backed off into the weeds of the creek bank and straightened out again, and the truck disappeared behind the tall corn.

Cleveland had not moved when the truck started backing off. The mules had jerked their heads up and tilted their ears forward, but they would not run, and Cleveland stood on the turnrow with his breeches legs almost brushing against the fender of the pickup as John Chaney backed it down toward the cornfield. He lifted a hand slowly to take the cigarette from his lips and hold it between thumb and forefinger while the smoke curled up from the shortening snipe, watching the white man back away in his truck without giving Cleveland a chance to say another word about whether he wanted to move or wanted to stay.

"Howcome that man says he didn't remember Bully and Daly was my folks?" Cleveland thought, standing there watching the truck disappear. Surely the white man could remember that Cleveland was Bully Webster's boy; and he knew that Ruby Lee was Book Turner's girl. Or else he thought about them only according to where they were and the work they did; maybe that was the only meaning they had for him and the only way he could place them in his mind. But in what other way did the man think about Ruby Lee? That's what Cleveland wanted to know—how else did the white man think about Ruby Lee?

Cul Sally came to the end of a row and stopped his team in the field that lay farther up the creek. "EEEE-yah!" he hollered. "That man ride that truck just like it was a wild horse. What he come down here to see about, Clevelan'?" Cul called.

"He just lookin' at the crops," Cleveland answered. He had

to lift his voice and shout, because Cul's field lay on the other side of his own and there was still another day's work to be done before he could narrow the unplowed width down to nothing.

Cleveland caught the Pete mule's bridle and made the mule lift his head from the cotton stalks on the very end of the row, where he had lowered it to nip at the top leaves. The collar had slipped, and Cleveland shoved it tight against the mule's shoulders before going back to the cultivator handles to take up the lines again and make the turn and head the team toward the opposite end of the field, with the cultivator feet straddling a new row.

"He didn't gimme no chance," Cleveland said to himself, "to ask him about getting away from here to go out yonder to Papa's place." He plowed on, wondering why it was the boss man would come down there to offer him a place somewhere along the Navasot'. It was a thing that did not make much sense to Cleveland. The white man did not want to keep him out here in the bottoms any longer than he could help, that was clear enough. But still he would not get rid of him; Chaney would not let Cleveland get away even for a couple of days.

"Howcome he didn't gimme no chance?" Cleveland asked. "I meant to say somethin' about it today, but he wouldn't let me talk. Howcome he didn't gimme no chance to tell him what I need to do?"

CHAPTER FIFTEEN

Cleveland completed his round and stopped the team again. He stood the width of three cotton rows below the place where, fifteen minutes earlier, John Chaney had waited in the truck. The mules breathed hard, and the red Pete mule blew through his nostrils and shook himself, rattling the harness and shaking loose a little blob of the sweat foam that had gathered between his hindquarters. The blue mule lowered his head to crop at a sprig of Johnson grass that grew at the end of the row, and Cleveland slowly lifted the rope lines from around his neck and hooked them over one of the handles of the cultivator. He broke the cultivator feet from the earth, where they straddled the knee-high, leafy plants, and turned to look back across the rows toward the tall field of corn that grew beyond and fenced in the patch of cotton.

Cleveland listened, feeling in the breast pocket of his jumper for the sack of tobacco, and heard the droning of locusts in the willow trees along the creek bank that lay beyond the turnrow, and heard the harness rattle on the mules as they shifted their weight to ease themselves, and heard Cul Sally shout to his team in the young cotton of his own field.

"I sho' to God heard that truck again," Cleveland said. A cigarette made, he twisted the end of it and placed it between his lips, then felt in his hatband for a dry match, still looking across the cotton rows toward the cornfield, still listening.

The sun stood now well past midday, and Cleveland felt his stomach growl. He had not gone to the house for dinner. He had unhitched his team and tied the mules where they could eat in the tall grass along the creek bank, and he had taken a big drink of water out of the jug that sat in the shade of a willow. Then he had stretched out under the tree and slept for almost an hour. Now the sun stood at the beginning of the afternoon, and Cleveland was beginning to feel hunger burning in his belly. He had hooked up and plowed only two rounds before John Chaney drove toward him across the ends of the rows, but the day was hot and still, and the mules breathed hard and their thighs became foam-spotted, and Cleveland's jumper stuck to his back.

He finished his cigarette and took up the lines. The mules turned, and the cultivator wheels were astride a new row. When he was halfway down the length of the field, Cleveland heard the truck growl once more. A touch of breeze blew from the south and it brought the sound of the starter whirring the motor, then the whine of the truck in low gear and a grating as the gears were shifted. A long cloud of reddish dust rose above the far edge of the cornfield and grew as the truck picked up speed along the road, out of sight, that ran through the fields between the headquarters buildings and the highway.

The team checked, and Cleveland stood watching the cloud of dust that showed where the road lay. He had only to turn his head slightly to look toward the roof of his house where it showed above the corn tassels. His lips moved slightly, but the mumbling noise in his throat did not become words. Then he bent and picked up a clod of dirt. He flung it at the hindquarters of the Pete mule. "Hum up 'air!" he roared, and the team lunged forward. Cleveland hung onto the cultivator handles, and the feet, swerving in the dirt, cut into the cotton row and plowed up a three-foot stretch of the plants, which leaned and toppled behind the cultivator as it went on toward the far end of the field.

Cleveland went back to the house about the middle of the afternoon, and there was but one piece of cold corn bread on the shelf. He mopped the sweat drops off his forehead and stepped into the cool shade of the kitchen, and when he opened the cupboard and looked on the shelf he could find only one piece of cold corn bread. There was that one piece, about as big as a man's hand, lying on a plate on the shelf. And Cleveland was hungry.

"One piece," he said aloud, "and that piece got ants on it." He reached out a big, rough-fingered hand and picked up the bread and held it so he could blow on it, scattering the little orange ants that came in a trail through the floor and up the side of the cupboard and marched around the edge of the plate the corn bread was on. The plate was all that there was left on the shelf—the plate and the ants.

Cleveland went over to the table and pulled up a chair and

sat down. He bit into the corn bread and chewed slowly while he looked out the kitchen door, which he had left open as he entered. A warm breeze blew in through the door, blowing from across the river, and the wind against Cleveland's blue denim jumper and against the waist of his overalls cooled the sweat so that when he leaned back and pressed the cloth against him it felt cold. In the middle of July it felt cold. Cleveland swallowed his corn bread and got up to drink a dipper of water out of the bucket that stood on the shelf by the kitchen door. The water was low in the bucket and it tasted of sulphur.

"And that's one more thing," Cleveland said. "The water bucket's nearly dry." He bent over a little so he could look out the kitchen door, and when he looked he could see the stand of cotton that ran toward the river. He could see his team standing in the barn lot with the harness still on the mules' damp backs, and he could see the line of willows and sycamores along the bank of the river, and the corn where it broke the line of cotton and stood high as a man on horseback. Everything outside was green and wavy, shifting and hazy, under the heat of the three-o'clock sun; and the locusts made so much racket in the trees along the river, all of a mile away, that the breeze brought the sound with it, and Cleveland heard it rising and falling and shifting until it was just as if the heat waves and the sound were the same thing.

Behind him the kitchen was quiet. It was cool and dim in the afternoon. The dishpan was dry and hung on the wall above the table. The stove was cold, and the dishes were clean and stacked on their shelf. The table was wiped clean except for the few crumbs that Cleveland had dropped, and among these a couple of the little orange ants already were running around. He turned away from the door and let his eyes get used to the dimness inside and then he walked toward the front part of the house. There was not a soul anywhere but Cleveland, and the house was quiet. The bed was made up and the floor was swept. The rocker and the straight chair sat on the front porch in the shade, and the frizzly hen and her twelve chickens were scratching in the dirt of the front yard. The rooster was chasing grasshoppers in the edge of the cotton field across the road that ran in front of the house. The road was red and dusty and empty, both ways, as far as Cleveland could see. The light was so bright it made the pupils of his eyes get small again, that quick, and he blinked at it, standing on the porch in the shade and looking up and down the hot red road.

"One God-damned piece of corn bread," Cleveland said, and he went around the outside of the house to unharness his team and let the mules wallow in the dust.

It was sundown before Ruby Lee came home. The light was red on the kitchen floor; the glow was beginning to fade while Cleveland sat there waiting. He heard her footsteps as she turned off the road into the yard and as she came around the outside of the house to the kitchen. The mules nickered when she walked by the barn lot. Just outside the kitchen door she stopped to take off her shoes and empty the dirt out of them, and then she stepped up onto the floor barefooted. Cleveland looked at her. She had her groceries in a flour sack that was about three-fourths full. As she put the sack on the table she turned toward Cleveland.

"The mules ain't been watered," she said. "They hangin' their heads over the fence tryin' to get out and get at some water."

Cleveland got up and crossed the floor toward her. His arm swung, and he slapped her in the mouth so hard that she fell against the wall and made the dishpan rattle on its nail. She shivered and stood there, still holding both shoes in one hand, while Cleveland moved toward her again. A little blood showed at the corner of her mouth. She backed along the wall to slide away from his upraised hand, and her eyes were wide and white.

"What for?" she said, with her breath so short he could scarcely hear her. "Don't hurt me again, Clevelan'. Don't come at me."

"Where you been? Howcome you been gone so long?"

"I come right back soon as I could," Ruby Lee gasped. "I been to the sto', and I walked back."

"Where else you been? What else you been doin'? It don't take all day to go to the sto'."

"I been to the sto'. I walked back," she repeated. Ruby Lee stood still, but the shoes dropped from her fingers and hit the floor as he moved toward her again.

"I heard the truck," Cleveland said. His arm lifted again. "I heard the man stop by here."

"Mr. John stopped after he seen you," she said. "He say he want me to go with him to town, that he need somebody to help out at the house." Ruby Lee's voice was little more than a whisper, and her eyes were large as they watched Cleveland. "I come on back as soon as I could. I told him I couldn't come there and work."

Cleveland had lowered his arm again, but he was still watching her and he was still tense. "Can't they get no help in town?" he growled. "Why does he want to come out here after you?"

Ruby Lee caught her breath and held it for what seemed like a long time before she answered the question. "They help laid off for a week," she said at last. "His wife gone out of town someplace and there wasn't nobody there but me." She tried to back closer to the wall as she finished speaking, and her left arm came up, seemingly of its own accord, to bend protectingly in front of her body. "Don't come at me, Cleveland," she begged. "Don't come at me."

She need not have spoken, because Cleveland remained standing where he was. He stood watching her while her arm lowered slowly to droop again at her side. His own fist relaxed, and without another word he turned and went out to the barn lot to feed and water the two mules. The blue mule and the Pete mule started nickering when they saw him come out of the kitchen door.

Ruby Lee stood for a full minute where she had backed when Cleveland started for her; she was quiet, scarcely breathing, squeezed against the wall while she looked toward the door where Cleveland had gone out. She heard him speak to the mules in the lot and heard the rattle of the ears of corn that he shucked and threw into the feed troughs. She moved to the table, leaving her shoes to lie on the floor, and emptied the groceries from her flour sack. She felt weak and empty, her mouth hurt her, and every time she had her back turned toward the door and the barn she was listening for Cleveland's footsteps coming across the yard. It was not until she was halfway through fixing supper that she was able to get her mind on what she was doing.

Her feet dragged wearily as she moved about the kitchen. Her dress was stained with perspiration at the armpits and across the back. Her hair was still made up into buns on her head in the way she liked to wear it when she went to town, but the arrangement was not so neat now. The pins were working loose and some of the strands of black hair were stringing out, as if she had been in a high wind. She did not hold herself erect. In her weariness she let her body sag, and that, coupled with her shortness, made her look heavier and older—a full-breasted, full-hipped, round-stomached woman. It was an indication of how she would appear ten years later, and now, at twenty, she had no right to look that way; but her foot-dragging tiredness kept her from doing anything about how she looked, or caring.

The mules were fed and watered, and the gap was open so they could get out and get a little grass in the patch next to the barn, but Cleveland stayed in the lot and rolled a cigarette and smoked it until he knew that supper was ready. He went back to the house then and did not say a word to Ruby Lee while he ate, and after he finished supper and smoked another cigarette he went to bed.

Ruby Lee made herself a pallet with a quilt and slept on the front porch that night, and the mosquitoes woke her up five times before daylight.

CHAPTER SIXTEEN

Cool and quiet along both sides of the river, the bottom lands lay flat under a lifting fog that made the sun big and red in the east. It was Friday morning. Just a slight breeze nodded the tops of the cotton stalks and carried the morning sounds a long way across the fields. Trace chains rattled on teams that moved along the turnrow road to cultivators and sweepstocks standing in the cotton. The damp smell of the river was in the air, a mixed smell of fish and willow roots, and one puff of breeze brought with it the sickly sweet smell of cotton worms. Ruby Lee woke with her shoulders cold and her hair wet from the fog, with the sun in her eyes and the smell of the river in her nostrils.

"Lawd God," she said, because she had slept so late and Cleveland had to have his breakfast before he went to the field.

But Cleveland was all right this morning. If he were not all right, then he showed no signs of the anger that had been in him the night before. He was moving around in the kitchen, making coffee, and the mules stood harnessed in the barn lot.

"I done been to the well," Cleveland said. "They a fresh barrel of water on the sled. But I wish to God we had some settled water to make coffee. That sulphur-water coffee ain't fit to drink."

"I meant to get water yestiddy," Ruby Lee said. "I meant to go, but it was so late when I got back from the sto'—"

Cleveland turned on her. His jumper was open, and his chest showed dark and wide above the bib of his overalls. "Don't say nothin' to me about yestiddy," he warned. "I ain't ready to talk about yestiddy." His eyes followed Ruby Lee as she went to the oilstove to light another burner.

She took the frying pan down from its nail and got eggs out of the bucket, and went to the cupboard to get the piece of salt pork. "Yo' breakfast be ready in a minute," she said. Even if Cleveland were all right she could not get rid of that uneasy feeling in her stomach. She got it every time she looked up and saw him watching her, and when she had her back turned on him she felt the skin crawl at the back of her neck. It was all she could do to eat a couple of bites of breakfast while Cleveland was finishing off three eggs, his coffee, the fried bacon, and some of the light bread that she had brought from the store.

"I'm goin' to be back here for dinner," Cleveland said. "I'm goin' to be hungry when I gets here."

"I ain't goin' nowhere," Ruby Lee told him. "I have yo' dinner ready."

The sun was already an hour high and turning hot, when Cleveland came to where his cultivator stood at the end of a cotton row. There were people in the fields ahead of him. Two teams moved across the middle of the replant cotton across the road, and Cul Sally was completing a round in his field, forty yards down the creek from Cleveland's cultivator.

He answered Cul's call with a grunt, and Cul lifted laughter into a shout. "You late to the field," Cul called. He turned his team and set the sweeps astride a new row of cotton. "How-come you ain't up early like the rest of us, Clevelan'?" he shouted, loud enough so the chopping hands could hear where they followed after the cultivators in the field across the turn-row road. He bent double with laughing. "Clevelan' been up all night triflin' with his wife!"

Cleveland slapped his team into a walk. "Never you mind, man," he said, not nearly loud enough for Cul to hear. "Never you mind." He plodded down the row, his head bent over and his eyes watching his work.

Cleveland was good with a team and a plow. The rows behind him were clean and neat. The cotton was dirted up carefully where Cleveland's cultivator had passed. The loose earth formed a ridge down the center of the row of cotton, covering the roots to keep them from the baking sun and smothering out the little new shoots of green grass that already had begun to push up through the crust. His sweeps ran close to the stalks, but seldom did he turn one under, and he plowed the ends of his rows clean. His arms were thick and heavy, but the muscles lay loose under the skin, and his plowing was effortless. "He's one of the best hands I've got," John Chaney had said early in the spring when he saw how Cleveland had moved in on the place left grassy by Walter Steptoe and cleaned it up and got a crop to growing green there despite the high water and the muddy fields. "I tell you, Cleveland is steady; he's a good man, and he keeps his house up," the white man had said. "That's one man I want to keep on my place."

It had been warm enough to plant cotton by the end of February, and Cleveland got a good stand. The spring rains were gentle, but there had been one washing rain in April that flooded the creek and backed it out over ten acres of low ground, where the replant cotton was now coming on and growing so fast it was almost catching up with the older planting.

John Chaney liked Cleveland's crop. After the ground dried off during the spring, the dust clouds that rose behind his truck would die down and vanish as he slowed to ride by Cleveland's fields and look out of the window to see how the cotton grew out all the way to the turnrow, and how the end rows were free of grass. He noticed how Cleveland went into the corn when it was tall and beginning to silk, to cut down all the Jimson weeds and cockleburs.

The white man took a liking to Cleveland and would stop his truck in front of the house and sit there with his wide-brimmed straw hat on the seat beside him so the breeze could blow across his forehead. He would sit wiping the dust from his red face with a big white handkerchief while he talked crops and weather with Cleveland.

Cleveland wished that Ruby Lee wouldn't be sitting in the rocker on the porch every time the boss man stopped by. He wished she would get up and go in the house and leave him to talk to John Chaney by himself, instead of having her there behind him on the porch sitting in the chair.

"You got a nice-looking wife, Cleveland," John Chaney said. "Can she cook?" He was laughing, his voice was high and his laughter shrill.

Cleveland had to grin. "Yassuh, she cook all right."

The boss man roared with laughter, looking toward the porch as he grated the truck gears together and went off down the turnrow road, leaving a cloud of fine dust to drift and settle slowly in the evening, covering the cotton leaves with an added film of red.

"I wish you wouldn't set on the porch all the time when I talk to the man," Cleveland told Ruby Lee. "I don't like to have somebody at my back listenin' to me talk."

Ruby Lee rocked in the chair, pushing against a roof post with a bare foot. "I don't pay you no mind," she said, rocking. "It's so hot in the house I like to sit out here in the evenin' where the air is cool."

Cleveland looked at her closely, how she sat in the chair and pushed against the roof post to rock herself. "What you wearin', woman?" he asked. "What you got on under that dress?"

"Nothin'," Ruby Lee said. "I just got on this old dress. It so hot today."

That was the first time Cleveland hit her. He slapped her across the face so hard that the chair tilted up on one rocker and nearly turned over. "You get in that house," he said. "You get off this porch."

It was then that Cleveland began thinking about the place on the Navasot' again, about how it had been there with Bully and Daly and Vincent and Tina and Hoodoo and Little Suster and Unca Dempse in the years that the crops were good and the river stayed low. It was then that he began worrying about the family again, and about having the two mules that Bully needed if he was ever going to make another crop.

"Us don't belong here," Cleveland said to Ruby Lee while the crop was still young, soon after the corn started silking. And after the white man began stopping regularly to talk to Cleveland in the field or at the house, Cleveland felt even more uncomfortable. "I don't know what the man want," he puzzled. "Is he so lonesome that he need to stop and talk with me?"

There was no denying that the boss man was interested in the crops; the land was his, and being interested in the crops on it was his business. And it was true enough that Cleveland was a new man on the place, but none of that was enough to explain to Cleveland why the white man spent so much time down there. The man had too much to do, he had too many places to go, too much acreage to cover, to spend so much time down there with a new man out of pure neighborliness. Cleveland knew John Chaney only as the boss man who drove the green pickup to the bottoms and rode the turnrow roads to keep close check on his workers. When the white man left the bottoms he was gone completely outside Cleveland's experience and imagination; Cleveland had no picture of how the white man spent his time in town.

He could have no way of knowing what moved the boss man —what emotions, what drives there were that kept John Chaney so constantly in the green pickup, riding the roads, bumping across pastures, overseeing work, making money to put into still more land and bigger crops, and seldom spending time at home. Seldom seeing his wife as more than a figure across from him at the supper table—sleeping in a separate room, leaving early in the morning.

Cleveland knew very little about John Chaney, but he was not alone in that ignorance. Joe Coby, who had been with the white man for years, knew little more. To all the people living in the broad bottom lands along the river, Chaney was the boss man, and that was all they needed to know. Beyond that he did not exist for them. They respected him in a way for his power over them, and at times they feared him; but as for mutual understanding, there was none. The people worked for him. He worked the people.

Cleveland could not name the feeling that came over him when John Chaney began to stop by the house. He did not like the way that the boss man looked at Ruby Lee, nor did he like the way that the white man would speak to her when she was with him in the field, calling her by name. A man could talk to his wife, they could play together, work, laugh, and make fun; but when the boss man came to the field the woman should be there merely as a figure in the background. She was there to do her work and not to speak. She might know as much about the crops and the weather as the man, but it was not her place to speak of it. It was her place to keep quiet and keep her head down and do her work and never notice that the white man was in the field.

To Cleveland a white woman was completely taboo. In town on Saturdays he would feel a vague discomfort and a nervousness if, on a crowded corner, a white woman should accidentally cross his glance with hers. Once when he was walking the highway toward town he had left the road and cut across a field to avoid passing a white woman waiting on the highway for help in changing a flat tire. He wondered little about how the white man thought, but he could not help believing that the taboo worked both ways.

To Cleveland, there was something uncomfortable in the air when John Chaney stopped by the house and spoke to both of them, or to Ruby Lee alone.

Cleveland began wondering then. There had been no such complications, no such strange and unpleasant discomfort, when he lived back on the Navasot'. "We don't belong out here," he told Ruby Lee. "It look like these bottoms too big for us, and I just as soon we could move somewhere else."

Ruby Lee had a practical mind. She came as near to understanding Cleveland as could anybody, and she knew him to be impulsive and quick in his thinking, though his body could move lumpishly slow. She knew him to be quick to get mad, but just as quick to laugh. He was changeable as a summer cloud and as full of lightning as a thunderhead, and his mind jumped ahead to what he wanted without ever thinking about the reality that lay between himself and his wishes.

"Clevelan'," Ruby Lee said patiently, reaching out a hand to touch him as they sat on the porch in the darkness. "Clevelan', the cotton ain't knee-high, and you talkin' about goin' off and leavin' it. I never heard of anybody leavin' a place before they crop was made."

Cleveland grinned at her, but he was stubborn. "I don't know," he said doggedly. "If I was to take a mind to do it, I might be the first one to go off and leave a crop."

It was something he could think about. In doing so he could feel himself free, independent, able to act as he wanted to act. He loved the crop and was proud of it; he made his farming an art. His strength made him more than the equal of the fertile ground that sprouted grass and weeds for him to kill; his ingrained, sure knowledge of planting and cultivation made the growth of a strong crop almost a certainty. He nursed the fine stand of corn and the gleaming rows of cotton, and his sweat salted the ground, but he could take a perverse pleasure in thinking about going off and leaving the crop to be choked by grass and smothered by vines. It was a feeling of pleasure akin somehow to that felt by a small boy who builds a tall house of dominoes, then in one sweeping blow of his fist sends the whole thing crashing to the floor. It was a mark of unreasoning immaturity and a perversity similar to the blind contrariness of the river, which made the land rich and able to bring a crop to full fruit, but which with a sudden flood could almost overnight destroy a year of a man's work and leave the bottoms stinking and slimy with the decaying remains of matured plants.

Had it not been for Bully and the family and the fact that they had no mule and had no way of making the land pay without a mule, Cleveland might not so readily have thought about abandoning his crop. But the place on the Navasot' was coming to represent for him a security that he had lost. He was forgetting the times of dry weather when the corn turned yellow and shriveled, and the floodwaters that came in the spring or stood on the lowlands during the fall and winter; he was remembering the good crops, the full years, and forgetting the debt that Bully had loaded onto himself in order to gamble seed on the making of a good crop.

The hold that the family had on him still was strong, and he could feel that his leaving had cut the foundation from under Bully's ability. Because the ability to farm and make the place had not been Bully's, but the family's. It took all of them working together. Vincent was no good alone, Hoodoo was still too young, Unca Dempse was done for, and Bully could not handle it by himself. Without a mule he could not hope to handle it. Daly, Tina, and Little Suster were female; they did not count.

"I wish I could get back out there," Cleveland said to Bully in town when they met in front of the bank when the Saturday crowd was thickest. "I wish I could get out there just for a couple of days to help you-all out. It look to me like if I got that team out there I could do a heap of good in a couple of days."

Bully laughed at his son. He was proud of the boy and glad

that he had a place in the bottoms and was doing well on it, but the boy didn't know. Bully shook his head. "I borrowed a team for a couple of days this spring and got a garden broke up for Daly, and that's about all I done. I been lookin' for a mule ever since, to try to get ground ready for a little bit of corn, but it's too late now to do much of anything. Lawd God, it would take a month to get that ground ready to plant."

"If I could get caught up I'd like to come out there," Cleveland said. "If I could get through to where the man would let me go for a while I'd like to take that team and bring it out and see what I could do. The way it is now it's all I can do to get in here to town on Sadday. We ride in here on the truck, and we got to be ready to go back when the truck leave. Lawd God, I don't know when I'll get to the end of that plowin'," he had said.

Cleveland could see the end of his plowing now. The blue mule and the Pete mule walked with their heads up and left the cleaned rows behind them. The morning passed quickly and the near edge of Cul Sally's field was coming closer. Cleveland unhooked the team and went to the house for dinner, but he stayed only long enough to smoke a cigarette after eating. The cool shade on the front porch was inviting, but he went to the barn and watered the mules before slipping their bridles back on and jumping up to the Pete mule's back to ride again to the field. He would be through by sundown. And tomorrow was Saturday. John Chaney wanted him in town to talk about moving in the fall. "I didn't get no chance to tell him yestiddy," Cleveland thought. "I couldn't get to say what I wanted to." But tomorrow he would go to town; tomorrow he would tell the boss man.

About three o'clock in the afternoon Ruby Lee came around the end of the cornfield and walked down the turnrow next to the creek bank. She had a pitcher of hot coffee in her hand. Cleveland wiped his face on the sleeve of his jumper and watched her walk toward him.

Ruby Lee was looking better today. Some of yesterday's

weariness and indifference had dropped from her, and she looked good even in the old dress that she had on and the old hat of Cleveland's that sat on the back of her head. She had on a pair of field shoes for walking in the hot dirt, but above the tops of the shoes her legs were strong and brown and smooth.

"I brought you a pitcher of coffee," she said. "Somethin' hot inside you will keep you from feelin' the sun so much."

Cleveland drank a big swallow from the mouth of the pitcher. The coffee was so hot it nearly scalded his throat going down, but it relaxed him and made him feel good. There was cream in it, and sugar, and the pitcher was warm in his hands.

He drank again. "Lawd God," he said, "I never had anything so good. Howcome you bringin' me coffee in the middle of the e'nin'?"

"The sulphur settled out of the water," Ruby Lee said. "You said you wanted some good coffee, and I thought I fix it up and bring you some."

"Where you get the cream to put in it? I didn't know we had milk at the house."

"Mr. John brought it," Ruby Lee said. "He stopped at the house and brought it in and said it would spoil in his truck. He said he got it at the sto' for his dinner and forgot about it. I used some of it in that coffee."

Cleveland looked at the coffee in the pitcher and then raised his head slowly to stare hard at Ruby Lee. He said nothing while he looked at her, but held the pitcher out at arm's length and turned it over. The coffee poured out on the ground. It splashed into the dirt and Ruby Lee felt the warm drops hit her legs. Cleveland held the pitcher upside down.

Ruby Lee watched the last slow drops fall from the rim of the pitcher. "You poured my coffee out," she said. "You don't want what I bring you."

"If I got to wait for the man to bring me milk for my coffee, I don't want no milk." He shoved the pitcher at her. "Take the pitcher. Take it back to the house when you go and wash it out. I don't want nothin' that the man bring on this place. The less I got to do with the man the better I like it." Cleveland turned around to the cultivator and took up the lines. He shouted at the mules.

Ruby Lee started back to the house. She swung the empty pitcher at her side with three fingers through the handle. By the time she got to the edge of the cornfield she was crying.

Cul Sally stopped his team in mid-field to shout at Cleveland. "Wish my wife was nice to me," he shouted. "Wish my wife would bring me somethin' to drink in the e'nin'. What she bring you in the jug, Clevelan'?"

Cleveland plowed on, making the mules step out in the re-plant cotton. He felt the sun burning down on the back of his neck and the sweat soaking his jumper, but with every round he could see the end of the field coming closer. He'd be done by sundown.

CHAPTER SEVENTEEN

Cul Sally ran chords on his guitar and laughed. He looked through the plate glass of the store window and laughed again, running his chords. "Herb Store" was what the sign said: it told about the roots and the powders and the lucky stones inside on the counters. It told about what the roots and the powders and the lucky stones would do. Cul Sally laughed while he read the sign, and he leaned one shoulder against the wall of the building next to the plate glass window and looked up at the people stopping in front of the store. "It look to me," he said, "like all they tryin' to tell is they got goofer dust for sale." The people around him laughed at Cul Sally and watched him picking at the strings of his guitar. He began to sing:

"I put ashes in my sweet baby's shoes . . ."

Saturday morning in town and already the streets were getting crowded. Plenty of money was loose in town while it was cotton-chopping time. The preachers roamed the streets to pick out a place where they could hold an afternoon meeting, looking for the best places while the day was still young and the streets not too crowded. The trucks were coming in from the bottoms, and the people started walking the streets, looking for a way to spend their money. The guitar players, finding themselves a good corner, already were making themselves the center of a crowd gathered to listen to the songs.

I would go to Dallas
To see the worly fair;
Lawd, I would go to Dallas,
But I'm afraid John Chaney be there.

Cleveland and Ruby Lee heard Cul Sally singing as they turned the corner from the street that led to the lot where the truck from John Chaney's place was parked. They had to shove to get through the crowd around the store window and the singer, and when they saw the lucky stones and the roots Cleveland caught Ruby Lee by the arm and said to her, "Let's get on from here. I got no time to waste lookin' at that foolishness."

Cleveland started laughing before they had walked more than half a block down the street. He laughed so hard he had to stop walking and lean over to beat one knee with his hand.

"What the matter with you, Clevelan'?" Ruby Lee asked. "What so funny that you about to kill yo'self?"

Cleveland straightened up. "I wonder do Mr. John know." He laughed again. "I wonder do the white man know they got his name on one of them roots down yonder in that window? I wonder do he know they got his name on somethin' that grow down in the ground?"

"They supposed to work," Ruby Lee said. "I heard it told

that John the Conqueror roots was good for somethin', but I don't know what they do."

John Chaney's black Plymouth sat in front of the bank. The car that he drove in town was clean and shiny, because his wife drove it most of the time while he roamed through the bottom lands in the pickup. She kept it washed and waxed, as carefully tended as her own hair, and most likely if she had not gone to Houston on the train John Chaney would have been driving his truck this morning. Cleveland saw the car sitting there in front of the bank while he was crossing the railroad tracks, and he walked faster, telling Ruby Lee to step up if she were going to walk with him.

"Yonder Mr. John in the bank," he said. "I'm goin' to tell that man now. I'm goin' to tell him we movin' off the place."

John Chaney came out the door of the bank before Cleveland and Ruby Lee got there, and the white man was getting into his car when Cleveland spoke to him.

"Good morning, Cleveland," John Chaney said, shutting the door and settling himself under the steering wheel.

"We just got to town, Mr. John. I come in to tell you about us aimin' to move."

"Well, that's good, Cleveland. When you get your crop made in the bottoms I'll see about getting you a better team."

Ruby Lee stood on the curb and looked at Cleveland while he talked to the boss man. Cleveland held his hat in his hand and had to bend over a little so that he could see John Chaney as the white man sat inside the car.

"I don't know as I can make no crop," Cleveland was saying. "We thinkin' about leavin' now, Mr. John. We thinkin' about movin' on off there right away."

John Chaney looked from Cleveland to Ruby Lee and then back at Cleveland again. "What you talkin' about, Cleveland?" he asked, his voice increasing in shrillness. "You ain't figuring on leaving me in the middle of the year?"

"I done finished plowin' that cotton. The crop ready to lay by; it won't be no trouble to make."

Chaney turned the key in the switch and stepped on the starter. The motor caught and the car purred. "I know it won't be any trouble to make," he said. "You're goin' to finish that crop with me, Cleveland. Who else would I put on there? Don't come to me this time of the year talkin' about leavin'. I'll move you when the time comes. I got a good place for you in the fall, but you know you can't go off now before that crop is gathered."

"I been thought about that, Mr. John, but it look like us got to go."

"This ain't the time of year for you to move," John Chaney said. "I've never had anybody leave me in the middle of the summer." He put the car in gear and started to back out of his parking place. "I'm goin' to come down there Monday mornin', and I want to find you in the field. You got to stick with that crop till it's done, and I don't know howcome you come talkin' to me like this."

Cleveland had to move while the boss man backed out. "I got no time to listen to you talk about leaving," John Chaney said, turning his head to look back over his shoulder for cars coming down the street. "You wait till Monday and see if you haven't changed your mind."

Cleveland stepped back on the curb and Ruby Lee looked at him. "You done told him," she said. "That man ain't goin' to let you leave him now. He ain't goin' to leave no crop not made."

"All us got to do is go," Cleveland said, watching John Chaney's black Plymouth go up the street and cross the railroad tracks. "He can't keep me there if I don't want to stay. I don't owe him no money."

"You owe him that crop," Ruby Lee said. "He put money in that crop."

Cleveland turned to face her. "I believe you just as soon

stay. I believe you like to stay." His voice was low and troubled with the idea of her wanting to stay, and his eyes narrowed to slits while he looked at her.

"We don't need no trouble with the white man," Ruby Lee said. "He been pretty good to us, Clevelan'."

"He been too good to us." Anger stirred in Cleveland's tone.

"He ain't cuss you, is he? He ain't work you too hard?"

"You a bitch, woman! You a white man's whore! You like what you doin'!" Cleveland forgot that he was standing in front of the bank; he forgot that there were people walking the streets. He would have hit her with his fist except for the fact that it was only the words that were new to him. The thought had been there, and now it came out.

"Be careful, Clevelan'. You in town," Ruby Lee said quickly. "You can't raise no fuss on the streets in town. Don't make no trouble," she begged. "Don't do no meanness when I tell you why I wish we stay on the place in the bottoms."

"Howcome?" Cleveland asked, still following out his thought about her. "Howcome you let the man come around? Howcome you a woman like this?"

Ruby Lee looked up at him with troubled eyes. One arm was stretched out toward Cleveland, the palm facing him as if to push him off and hold him away if he started toward her. "Who goin' to stop him? You ain't goin' to—he the boss. You been heard what kind of a man he was—everybody been heard what kind of a man he was. And I don't want to cause no trouble." She caught hold of Cleveland's arm. "I don't want there to be no trouble now, Clevelan'. I want us to stay there without no trouble. The man won't come back; he won't bother us none, and I don't want us to start no trouble with him." She held on to Cleveland's arm and shook it a little as she talked.

"I ain't told you, Clevelan'—I didn't want you to make no fuss. I wanted to wait till I was sure, but now I know. I knowed for sure when I got so sick after walkin' all the way back from town yestiddy." Her eyes were wide, looking at Cleveland. Her face was set and intense. "Us goin' to have a baby, Clevelan', and I want us to stay there without no trouble." She stopped. She had spoken fast and low, and now she was out of breath. Her hand dropped away from Cleveland's arm and she stood there watching him.

Cleveland looked at his wife. She was young and pretty. Her hair was done up in the way she liked to wear it when she came to town on Saturday. Her dress was good, and Cleveland knew it was good, because he went with her when she bought it right after they were married. It cost him fifteen dollars, but Cleveland let her have the money, because he wanted his wife to look right, not like a field hand. The dress fit her tightly and followed the curve of her shoulders and the swell of her breasts, and it was snug about her waist.

Cleveland liked that dress. It had made him feel proud of his wife and of himself, like he was getting somewhere, like life was something more than the cotton field and the turnrow road. But now he looked at Ruby Lee's face and did not like the prettiness there. He did not like her good looks and the tight fit of her dress. Bitterness welled up in him and flooded through all his body. His fist doubled itself slowly and then relaxed, and words came to his lips. He hit her with words instead of a swinging fist.

"Whose baby it goin' to be?" he asked. "Whose baby it goin' to be?" And he turned his back on her and walked away, leaving her to stand there looking after him.

CHAPTER EIGHTEEN

"I get to thinkin' about Clevelan'," Bully said. "I get to thinkin' about him and Ruby Lee and it worry me. I don't like what I hear about the way they makin' out in those bottoms."

"Cleveland goin' to do all right," Daly said, though her voice sounded as if she were trying to reassure herself as much as convince Bully. "The boy still young, and he hardheaded, but this just his first year out there, and I believe he do all right."

Breakfast was over and Unca Dempse and the children had gone to the front of the house. Tina had taken a gallon syrup bucket and talked Vincent into going toward the creek with her to look for wild grapes, and Hoodoo and Little Suster were playing around outside while Unca Dempse sat on the front porch and sucked on the short stem of his pipe.

Bully had started out to the barn, intending to patch a chicken coop that stood against the lot fence, but he turned back and came into the kitchen where Daly was washing the dishes.

"It's been almost a month since I last seen him in town," Bully said, shifting on his feet and stepping aside to keep out of Daly's way. He was so seldom in the kitchen when she was working there that he felt uncomfortably out of place, slightly deferential. The house was Daly's domain, the barn and the fields were his. "He said then he was doin' all right, but the boy wasn't satisfied. He kept talkin' about comin' back out here."

Daly grunted and plunged her hands into the dishpan. She rattled the pans in the warm, soapy water. "I wish he'd stayed out here," she said. "If him and Ruby Lee had to get married, I wish they had come on out here and helped with the place."

Bully watched her as she scrubbed viciously at the pans. Her back was to him as she bent over the table. She worked quickly, with her dress tight across her back between the shoulders as she soused the pans and scraped at them, churning the water almost as much as she would when she was washing out clothes on a scrubboard. She stepped to the stove for a dirty pan and back to the table again, never bothering to look at Bully, but keeping her eyes on her work and talking straight ahead of her.

Her tongue was sharp this morning. It was Saturday, and Hoodoo kept asking why they couldn't go to town, and she had slapped him at the breakfast table. She had lashed out at

Bully when he sided with the boy, and even Unca Dempse got his share of her bitterness when he looked up from his plate and asked, "Howcome they can't be less quoilin' at the table?"

Bully was in the kitchen now to try to make his peace with her. His voice was conciliatory, even though he disagreed with what she said. "You know they wasn't nothin' to keep Clevelan' here. The house too little for him and Ruby Lee to move out here after they married. I don't know what the matter is, but the boy ain't satisfied, else he never would have talked to me about comin' back." Bully looked around for a seat, but Daly had seized the broom and shifted the chairs to begin sweeping. Instead of sitting down he moved to the kitchen door and stood looking out toward the barn.

"Mr. John said he don't know about Clevelan'," Bully said from the door. "When I talked with the man yestiddy he said Clevelan' been actin' pretty wild. He said he hope he don't get in trouble."

"Cleveland young," Daly said. "He act up, but he ain't mean."

Bully waited a moment before speaking again, and then his words were not in answer to Daly's comment. "I wish," he said, "I wish I could have seen Clevelan' and talked with him before Mr. John stopped by here yestiddy."

"You could have seen him," Daly said. "You could have gone out to the bottoms."

"I could have walked out there, but it would take me all day. And the boy busy; he got his crop to make. I don't want to worry him."

"The white man would give you a ride." Dust rose from the floor ahead of Daly's broom. "Get out the door. Let me sweep out this kitchen." She hardly waited for Bully to step out of her way. "The white man come by here all the time. He would let you ride with him out there. You goin' to ride in to town with him next week, ain't you? He ain't too proud to let you ride in the truck with him."

"I don't know," Bully said. "I hate to worry the boy."

Hoodoo came around the corner of the house. He had on nothing but a pair of small blue overalls. His bare feet left tracks in the dust where he walked in the shadow of the house. The skin on the soles of his feet was tough, and it was too early in the morning for the dirt in the unshaded portion of the yard to be hot, but Hoodoo had burnt his feet in sun-heated sand too often, and the keeping to the shade of the house was a habit with him. He saw Bully standing by the back door and looked cautiously to see if Daly were where she could hear him.

"Ain't us goin' to town, Papa?" he asked. "Us ain't been in there on Sadday for a long time. Howcome we can't go to town this e'nin'?"

Daly heard him and opened her mouth to tell him to hush, but Bully walked away toward the barn, telling the boy to follow him. "We got too much to do here," Bully said. "It ain't no use in all us tryin' to walk in there this e'nin'. You quit askin' about goin' to town, else yo' mama goin' to get hold of you and wear you out. You don't need to worry about goin' to town."

"Won't Mr. John be back today?" Hoodoo asked. "Wouldn't he let us ride in with him in the back of the truck?"

"He might," Bully said. "But I ain't goin' to ask the man. He too busy. He got too much to do to fool with haulin' us to town when they ain't nothin' we could do when we got there. I let you go with me when I go in to pay off the note at the bank. I reckon maybe I be goin' in there next week. Mr. John say he let me ride in with him then."

That satisfied Hoodoo for a while, and he turned to run back across the yard toward the front of the house, where he and Little Suster had been playing. "Br-r-r-d-n!" said Hoodoo, backing and turning. "Br-r-r-d-n. Dah! The man sho' drive that truck. Lawd, I wish I could ride in the green truck with Mr. John."

In the barn lot Bully straightened a couple of rusty nails with his hammer and turned the chicken coop on its side. He drove the two nails to secure loose planks, and the coop was sturdy again. The work was done in little more than a minute, but the air in the barn lot was still, with the house cutting off the slight breeze, and when Bully stood up again he was perspiring. He felt tired, and the sun was uncomfortably hot to him, though there had been days when he had longed for a morning as cool as this. A lassitude had come over him and left him without energy or the desire to work. The lot fence sagged in several places, and Bully stared at them while he held the hammer in his hand, but he made no move toward fixing the fence. He seemed mentally to shrug his shoulders as he tossed the hammer to the top of the chicken coop and reached into his back pocket for the paper-wrapped plug of tobacco.

This year made twenty that Bully had been on the place. The land belonged to Unca Dempse, and Daly was reared there, but Bully had worked the place for so long now that he felt it was his. Bully had been working in town when he and Daly were married, but Unca Dempse had hated to see the last of his children leave him. "I make a deal with you, Bully," Dempsey Jefferson had said. "If you come out there and help me farm it, the place will go to you-all when I die. I got the team and the gear, but that place gettin' too much for me to farm by myself now that all the chillun done married and gone off."

"I wish I could start farmin'," Bully had told his father-in-law. "I don't like to stay in town. It don't seem right for me not to be out workin' with the ground."

Bully had been born out in the Brazos bottoms. He had grown up there and worked in the fields until he came to town and started working in the seed house at the oil mill.

"I wish us could get out there," he said. "Seem to me like I rather farm than stay in town."

Dempse had laughed. "You all right, Bully," he said. "You make a good farmer, and that's good land out there on the river. The house big enough. Nobody but me and Christine there. You and Daly and the baby could move out and we farm that place on halves. One of these days I ain't goin' to be able to work it no longer, and then you have the land."

It was a good place. Forty acres down along the river were of thick black soil, almost as rich as that of the red bottom lands along the big Brazos which lay fifteen miles away to the west. Spring Creek bordered down the south side of the farm. Coming back up toward the hill the land rose and was sandy where the house sat at the side of the road which led through the bottoms, roughly following the course of the river, now not five hundred yards from it, and again a mile away. The road ran north and south and the house faced east, with a yard that separated the front porch from the edge of the road by fifty feet.

So Bully had started farming. He had learned how to work out in the bottoms along the red Brazos. He was good to the mules, but he knew how to keep them walking. He knew how to make them do a day's work. He and Daly and Dempse and Daly's mother could keep the cotton chopped out, and at picking time they were enough to get the crop in before the rains spoiled it or the winter floods caught it. After Christine died and was buried at the Green Valley cemetery, the baby was getting big enough to work. Cleveland could do his part in the fields. Paul and Lully had died too young ever to be of any help, but then Vincent and Tina came on. The three-room house was more crowded, but after Christine was gone Daly and Bully had the front room to themselves, and they slept in there with the youngest child, and Cleveland and the rest of the children slept in the side room with Dempse.

The house seemed to grow smaller as the children came on, but still it held them, and with the family growing larger Bully could work the place and make it pay. It cost more to buy groceries and to keep the children in shoes and overalls, but they gathered good crops in the years they managed to stay ahead of the river. The river was there, and Bully dreaded it;

but he had to gamble on it, since it was the river that caused the richness of the land.

"The land rich; it got the strength in it," Bully thought to himself as he tucked his chew of tobacco into his cheek and leaned against the sagging lot fence. "But that don't make no difference this year."

He looked across the slope of the pasture toward the weed-grown fields, seeing the few upright cornstalks that remained standing between the pasture fence and the thick growth of trees that marked the beginning of the jungle matted along the turns of the river. The July sun was hot in the morning, and the growth of weeds and grass was heavy in the fields where there should have been a thick stand of cotton. But there was no cotton. There was no hay in the barn, no corn in the crib, and the fields lay untouched by a plow.

If there had been corn maybe the Beck mule would not have died. Maybe he could have made a crop this year. Maybe he could have got some seed in the ground and worked the land and made a crop before the river flooded again. But Bully shook his head and, leaning forward, spat carefully at a dried, dirt-caked corncob that lay just outside the lot fence. He felt the same way every year when the river got him, and it could not keep on forever. One or the other of them had to win and make an end to it.

It was the river that caused Bully to be fooling around the house on Saturday morning with nothing better to do than patch chicken coops, kill time, and wait for the white man to come by. The river lay behind his thinking about Cleveland; and his worrying about the boy out there in the bottoms not getting along too well with the white man, not getting along too well with anybody. Bully felt that part of the fault was his own for not having whipped the river and won out, for not having kept the place up and made it so that he would have something to offer Cleveland to keep him there.

"I wish I could have seen Clevelan'," Bully said again, "before I started talkin' to the white man."

In the front yard Hoodoo was still shouting and playing, making out that he was driving Mr. John's green pickup. "This one Sadday us goin' to stay out here all day," he told Little Suster. "But Papa say us goin' to town next week."

CHAPTER NINETEEN

The sky was red in the west. The sun was going down behind the store buildings and the houses and the trees that lined the streets in town. Chimney swifts squeaked and fluttered in the air over the tops of the buildings, clouds of them swarmed in the warm evening air, and above the chimney swifts a lone bullbat circled and rose higher.

"I been to the river and I been baptized," Cleveland shouted happily. "Lawd Jesus God! It's good enough for me."

Along the paved sidewalks of the street that ran by the railroad Cleveland went his way, singing and shouting. He was happy to the world.

"Lawd Jesus God!" Cleveland shouted while he put his feet one in front of the other along the hard pavement. "I'm happy and I don't care who knows."

All up and down the street the people stopped to watch Cleveland pass. They came to the doors of the cafés and shine parlors to see him walk the street in the evening while the sun went down.

"Ha' mercy," said Cul Sally's wife. "Cleveland's drunk again."

Cleveland paid no attention to the people along the sidewalk and in the doors of the cafés and hamburger stands. He paid them no mind when they called to him.

"Good e'nin', Clevelan'," Cul Sally called.

"Yee-e-e-e-e-whoo-oo-oo!" Cleveland shouted. "Lawd Jesus God."

Buddy Boy Taylor stood in front of a car parked at the curb, and he called to Cleveland passing by. "Who you mad at now, Clevelan'? Where yo' knife?"

"My knife in my pocket," Cleveland shouted. "But you can't fight Satan with no knife. I'm happy bound to whip sin out of the world."

The people laughed from the doorways while it got dark and Cleveland went his way. "Somebody ought to give him a pulpit," they said. "He's preachin' from the middle of the street."

"Amen!" thundered Cleveland as he turned the corner. "Amen," he sang.

Cleveland walked without staggering, his big feet coming down solid on the pavement, his arms swinging at his sides. His shirt flapped open over his chest where his ribs showed beneath the tight skin. He had no hat on. His hair was cut high in front, standing in a pyramid over his forehead, and the rest of his head was clipped close. His eyes were wide open, and he walked looking straight ahead. His white teeth showed when he opened his lips to shout and sing and laugh to himself. He walked with his shoulders back and his arms like swinging singletrees.

"I got a wife in town," he said. "I got a no 'count woman somewhere in this town, and I'm happy bound to whip sin out of the world." His hand went to his pocket and came out with his long-bladed knife. He pressed a catch on the handle and the knife blade flipped open and shone dully in the light that streamed out from the café doors and shone from the street lamps. The people faded back and left a clear path for Cleveland to walk in.

Cleveland crossed the street and the railroad tracks, looking for the Bon Ton Café, which stood down there across the railroad by a cotton warehouse, and when he got there he opened the double screen doors and walked to the middle of the floor.

"I'm lookin' for my wife," he shouted. "I'm lookin' for my woman. I know I got a woman here."

Sugar Davis ran the café, and Sugar didn't want any trouble on her place. "Ruby Lee done gone," she said from behind the counter. "Ruby Lee been here today, but she done left, Clevelan'. She done gone on down the street."

"I'm lookin' for my wife," Cleveland said. "It's time for me to take my woman home." He turned to look around him at the people slowly moving back. The knife gleamed while Cleveland held it in his hand.

"It's time for you to come with us, Cleveland," a white man said from the door, and the sheriff and two of his deputies walked into the café and closed in on Cleveland. "You done raised enough hell in town tonight, and it's time you come with us." The sheriff was laughing while he talked to Cleveland; his voice was friendly. "We been lookin' for you, Cleveland. Somebody's liable to hurt you while you're drunk."

The two deputies had their forty-fives on their hips, and they watched while the sheriff talked to Cleveland.

"Good e'nin', Mr. Jim," Cleveland said to the sheriff. "Me and my wife just fixin' to leave."

"Drop that knife, Cleveland. Drop it on the floor," the sheriff said. The knife slid from Cleveland's hand and thudded point-first into the wood floor. It stood there quivering. "You're a country boy, Cleveland," the sheriff said, "and I wouldn't want you to get hurt in town on a Saturday night. You better come with us." He put his foot against the knife and pushed. The floor splintered and the knife fell over. The sheriff stomped on it with his heel and the blade broke in two. "You better come with me. Mr. John asked me to take care of his niggers tonight."

"I'm happy tonight, Mr. Jim," Cleveland said. "Ain't causin' no harm. I just tryin' to find my wife and take her home."

"Bring him on," the sheriff said to his deputies, and they

caught Cleveland by the arms—one on one side, one on the other—and he had to go. He set his feet at the doorway to stop and holler "Amen!" one more time, and the deputy who had Cleveland's right arm pulled a forty-five and clipped him behind the ear with the barrel, and there was Cleveland, dragged to the sheriff's car like a sack of oats.

Mr. John came down to the jail with the sheriff to let Cleveland out on Monday morning. "Howcome you want to cause me all this trouble, Cleveland?" John Chaney asked. "Howcome you want to get in jail and cost me money to get you out?"

"I guess I got a little drunk Sadday night," Cleveland said. "I guess Mr. Jim had to take me in."

"Because you had that knife in your hand I had to pay five hundred dollars to get you out on bond, Cleveland," John Chaney said. "You goin' to have to raise a lot of cotton for me to pay off that bond, so you come on now and get in my truck and let me take you out to the bottoms. You don't want that crop to get in the grass."

"Wish you'd stay out of my jail, Cleveland," the sheriff said. "You eat too much. Mr. John ain't goin' to be this good to you and get you out another time."

"Nawsuh, Mr. Jim," Cleveland said. He got in the truck and John Chaney got in on the other side.

The boss man grated the gears together and the pickup roared down the street. Cleveland sat still in the seat while the white man drove. He stared straight ahead through the windshield, sitting as far away from the boss man as he could while they headed out of town toward the bottoms.

CHAPTER TWENTY

Sweat running down the black skin of Cleveland's face scoured it, and muddy drops of the sweat dripped from the end of his nose. The sun was halfway down in the west, and ragingly hot.

There was no wind. "I be damn'," Cleveland said. "I be damn' if I want to let that man set in his truck and cuss me while I sweats my guts out in this cotton."

Cul Sally's team was stopped on the turnrow next to Cleveland's, and Cul was leaning against the handles, laughing. "The matter with you, Clevelan'," he said, "you been up too late last night. You must stay out walkin' the turnrow road all night long. What the matter? Won't yo' wife come home?"

Cleveland spat on the ground and dipped his head to wipe his face with a shirt sleeve. He mopped at the end of his nose and then blew it by holding his thumb against one nostril and then the other.

"Mr. John ain't cuss you no worse than he cuss the rest of these niggers," Cul Sally said. "All he say is he say this cotton got to be got out of the grass and he don't want no nigger friggin' around till he ain't fit to work."

"I be damn'," said Cleveland. "Mr. John don't own me. I can come and go like I wants to."

"He don't own you," Cul said, "but he damn near do when you owe him a bill of money."

Cul turned his team down another row and followed the cultivator toward the line of trees that marked the far end of the field.

Cleveland turned his team and swung his cultivator handles around and straddled the cotton row with the sweeps and then stopped the mules and stood there, the knotted rope lines about his neck. He propped himself against the cultivator handles and looked around him, up and down the turnrow, over the cotton field that shimmered with heat waves, and at the choppers farther down the road. Far across the fields where the road led out of the bottoms, he saw the long streak of a smoking dust cloud rising behind Mr. John's pickup truck as the white man headed back toward town.

Cleveland watched the dust until it spread and thinned and settled in the still air. And then he lifted the knotted lines over his head and dropped them.

Under the midafternoon sun he unhitched his team and led it down the turnrow.

His cultivator stood next to the turnrow road at the edge of the big field where the boss man had all his teams working.

The white man had Cul Sally there plowing the big field. He had Buddy Boy Taylor, who was a truck driver, out there in the field with a cultivator and a team. And he had sent Cleveland to help get the cotton out of the grass.

"You've been through that place by the creek once," he said. "You've got that plowed out to where it'll be all right. I want you to get over there with those mules and take in behind Cul. Those choppers are going to move into that field tomorrow, because I want to have that cotton gone through before it starts to rain."

It was Wednesday, and he had been plowing there two days now. Every day it was sun, dust, and sweat, and the pair of mules pulling the cultivator. He had to be up early, because the boss man came to the bottoms by sunup, and he had his straw bosses riding through the fields on their horses, because that cotton wouldn't wait. The cotton didn't wait for sleep. Neither did the grass and the rain, and neither did the red flatland of the bottoms.

It seemed to Cleveland there was nothing left but the bottoms and the day-long plowing while the white man rode his truck down the turnrow road and shouted at a man when he caught him stopped to let his mules blow. Monday morning, when Mr. John got him out of jail, seemed like it was a year ago. He had seen nothing but the fields and the far line of trees along the bank of the Brazos since the white man had brought him back to the bottoms. Ruby Lee was gone; she hadn't come back to the house, and he couldn't tell whether he was glad or sorry. He tried not to think about her, because every time he thought it made him mad. He fixed his own breakfast and his own dinner and his own supper and tried not to think about her.

He ought to be glad she was gone—he ought to be glad she had not been there when the white man took him back to the house. He could not think straight then—he'd have hit her, he'd have beat her in the face with his hand, hit her, hit her till she fell to the floor—he'd have killed her like he wanted to do Saturday night when he was drunk.

But Ruby Lee was not there, and he was glad now because he knew that the fault was not hers. He had got it mixed up in his mind somehow, and the fear he felt, the insecurity, the distrust, had surged up to become something uncontrollable—a burning, hating, hurting flood of feeling that directed itself toward Ruby Lee instead of the white man, and she was the one who felt the weight of it all. He was glad she was gone; he was glad she hadn't been there, because now he knew his fear for where it lay, and the boss man, the white man and his pickup truck stood clear in his mind.

Cul Sally's cultivator reached the end of another row, swung around, and stopped close to the one Cleveland had left standing. "Clevelan'!" Cul shouted. "You sick?"

But Cleveland didn't answer.

The chopping gang stopped with their hoes in mid-air, and all the choppers raised their heads to watch Cleveland leading his team down the turnrow. "Where he goin'?" asked one. "It ain't quittin' time."

Cleveland took his mules home. He turned them in the lot and watered them and put corn in the troughs for them. He stood in the lot to look toward the house as it sat, empty and quiet, between the cotton field and the road.

"This make twice," he thought, "twice that I done come back in the middle of the e'nin' and seen the house empty." Ruby Lee was gone; he need not go in and sit there waiting, feeling afraid of something he was unable to name. Where she was he didn't know; her folks were there with the chopping gang. She might have gone to stay with somebody in town. But she was not here, and she was not anywhere close to John Chaney. The white man would have no time to bother her now.

He went to the yard and dipped a drink of water out of the water barrel that stood on the sled, and then, without going into the house, he started walking the road toward the distant place where it left the river bottoms and joined with the concrete highway that ran in to town.

Cleveland thought little about where his feet were carrying him. He let them walk where they wanted to walk, and without his thinking about it or planning it out clearly in his mind, they carried him down the turnrow road toward the place on the Navasot', fifteen miles away. He could not have said why it was that he wanted to go home, and he did not know what it was he was going to say to Bully when he got there, but his feet stepped out on the narrow red road—on the hard, hot dirt, carrying him away from the fields along the Brazos, carrying him away from the white man's fields.

The faded blue shirt on his back was open three buttons down from his throat and pinned in the middle with a safety pin. Rotten from caked sweat, it was split down the back and on the shoulders. His powerful muscles moved under it; his black skin shadowed itself beneath it. His round, close-clipped head was thrust forward above his shoulders. His arms were big and round as carved pieces of stovewood, and pink-palmed hands with stiff fingers, whitened by callouses, swung at his sides.

Go back, was what his feelings told him. Back to the place on the Navasot' where he had worked with the family, where the work, at least, had been his, and the good it did was for him and for the family. The fields along the Brazos were too big. The bottom lands were part of a system that took his work and merged it with the work of all the others in the plowing gang—the truck drivers, the choppers, and in the fall the cotton pickers—all the hundred others, until it lost its shape and its form and its individuality and was no longer his, but the white man's. He worked and he lived, but the crops that he raised could not be counted his. What he made would go back into the earth so that he could plant and make again, but none of it for him, all of it for the white man. The revolt that grew in Cleveland formed itself with roots deep back in feelings that were only half known, not yet formed into thought, not yet put into words. Nothing was his own, not even the mules that he had bought and paid for. He had to take them and go wherever he was sent. And his wife? Not even Ruby Lee. You couldn't make trouble with the white man. Maybe she could not help herself, or maybe she thought she was helping Cleveland by not making trouble. But what the man wanted he took, and that was the end of it. It all belonged to Mr. John, everything, and how was he to escape the circle that month after month and year after year would bring him back to where he started?

Go back, was what his feelings said, go back to the place on the Navasot' where you lived as a person, where the ground knew the mark of your feet and the house knew the sound of your step. Go back to where you belonged to the family and to yourself, because now in these big fields along this red river you belong only to the boss man.

And his feet walked where they wanted to walk, but still Cleveland knew that it was no use. His feelings told him wrong, because there was no going back. The earth that his feet had marked, that his plow had furrowed, was washed away by the winter floods, taken away and lost in the red, running river. The walls of the house could not echo forever the sound of his footsteps, and once he had left the place, once he had left the land, there was no going back to it. The time was gone, and he was gone with it. But still his feet took their own way down the narrow road of the red bottoms. Go back, they told him, leave the Brazos and the white man's fields.

CHAPTER TWENTY-ONE

An hour later Cleveland reached the highway. The boss man was gone to town, the turnrow road had been empty, and he had not met a soul. Now he stood at the edge of the pavement and waited for a ride. A truck slowed and stopped, and he got in without speaking to the driver, and they rode that way, not talking, all the way to town. When Cleveland left the truck he walked the back streets until he crossed town and started out the road toward the place on the Navasot'. He didn't stop to look for Ruby Lee. He didn't want to look for her now; he wanted to get back and ask Bully what to do.

The sun was dipping, and as it sank a breeze came up and cooled him while he walked. By the time he got to Spring Creek the sun had been down thirty minutes and the light was fading from the sky in the west, and the bullbats that he had heard earlier were gone from the air over the treetops.

Bully was sitting on the porch when Cleveland turned from the road into the yard. "Good e'nin', Papa," Cleveland said.

"Lawd God," said Bully. "Daly, here Clevelan'! Boy, what you doin' out here in the middle of the week?"

There was the sound of moving feet inside the house as Daly came to the door. "Ha' mercy," she said, moaning a little as she saw Cleveland. "Ha' mercy, Lawd."

Bully moved across the porch to stand in front of Daly and the door. He looked down at Cleveland waiting in the yard. "What is it, boy?" he demanded. "What you doin' comin' home in the night like this?"

Cleveland sat on the edge of the porch and leaned back slowly to stretch out on the floor. He extended his arms beyond his head and exhaled softly. He moved his feet where they hung over the edge of the porch as he felt his muscles begin to lose their tenseness. "I tired, Papa," he said. "I come clear from the Brazos this e'nin'."

"Tell him, Daly," Bully said. "He all right—he ain't goin' to cause no trouble."

"You ain't goin' to do no meanness?" Daly asked. "You didn't come here to make no fuss?"

"He all right," Bully said. "Leave him alone and tell the boy."

Cleveland sat up. "Tell me what?" he asked. "What I'm goin' to make a fuss about?"

"Ruby Lee here," Daly said. "She in the house." Daly stayed in the door, watching Cleveland. "But don't you hurt that girl—don't you make no fight with her."

"Howcome she here? When she come out here? I thought she stayed in town." He stood up and started toward the door.

Bully moved closer to him. "You ain't goin' to do no meanness," Bully said. "I ain't goin' to let you do no meanness."

Cleveland shook his head. His arms drooped from bent shoulders. "I ain't mad with her," he said. "I can't stay mad with her. Where is she? I want to talk with her."

"I here in the house," Ruby Lee said from the room behind Daly. Daly stood aside and Cleveland saw her now as she stood where she could look out and talk to him. "I come out here Sadday night. I walked out from town after you went off."

The dim light that came through the door was barely enough to show her form, to outline her against the shadowed room. A lamp in the kitchen threw a yellow glow on the walls of the front room, leaving Ruby Lee in silhouette, with the light that came from outside just touching her enough to show her face and her form as she waited, still half scared to come closer to the door. She was barefoot and she had on one of Daly's dresses. The dress was too big for her, and it left her looking shapeless, but in the darkness her figure already was indistinct.

Her voice was low and soft while she explained. She made her voice try to reason with him. "I didn't want to go back out to the bottoms then," she said. "I come here to stay with yo' folks, Clevelan'. Mama and Papa and them in the bottoms, and I come out here to stay with yo' folks."

"That girl walked all the way out here Sadday night," Daly said. "She walked all the way out here by herself. She been sick, Cleveland; she ain't been feelin' well in the mornin's. Don't you go fussin' and fightin' with that girl. You quick to get mad, Cleveland, but you watch what you say."

"He ain't goin' to start no meanness," Bully said, standing close to Cleveland. "You goin' to have me to monkey with, boy, if you want to start meanness."

"The baby yours, Clevelan'." Ruby Lee was no longer afraid. She was telling him; she was trying to make it all right with him. "I swear to God the baby yours, Clevelan'."

Dullness settled over him again and rooted him to the spot where he stood. "You talk to me about the baby," Cleveland said heavily. "You talk to me about that when I don't want to hear it. I been seen the man, I been heard the truck, I been wait for you to come home."

"Ha' mercy, Lawd," moaned Daly.

"Don't make no fuss," warned Bully. "Unca Dempse in there asleep, and you have them chillun runnin' out here in a minute."

Neither Cleveland nor Ruby Lee heard them. "I tell you the truth, Clevelan'." Ruby Lee came out of the room and stood close to him, looking up. "Hit me now, hit me in the mouth, but I tellin' you the truth. The baby yours, Clevelan'—I swear the baby yours. The man come there and he want to, but I don't let him touch me. He took me to his house when his wife was gone, but he couldn't make me stay there; he didn't stop me when I walked out and left." She looked little, lost, in Daly's dress. With her feet bare she was short. She came up no higher than Cleveland's shoulder. But she looked up at him; she turned her head back to look up at his eyes.

"You won't listen to me when I try to talk to you," she said, beginning to cry. "I can't tell you nothin' without you get mad and start to hit me. But the baby yours—I swear the baby yours. He never been able to touch me. I don't want to make trouble with the man for you, but I keep him away. He come back, he come back every day, but he don't touch me. I swear the baby yours." Her voice broke. She could not keep talking, nor continue looking up at Cleveland. Her head dropped, but she cried so softly to herself that the porch might have been empty, so still they stood, so silently grouped in the darkness that had thickened and turned black with the fading of the glow from the sky where the sun went down.

Then Daly moved. "Ha' mercy, Lawd," she said, reaching out for Ruby Lee. "Come in the house," she said. "Come and lie down on the bed. Cleveland ain't goin' to make no fuss."

Cleveland drew in his breath. He moved, remembering his feet. He felt the tiredness in his legs again. He heard Daly talking to Ruby Lee inside the room. But the dullness still weighted him, bore down on him so heavily he could not think.

"What you goin' to do, boy?" Bully asked at his side. "Set down and rest and tell me what you goin' to do."

"I done left the white man," Cleveland said. "He might come lookin' for me, but I done left him today."

"You owe him money," Bully said. "You owe him money from that trouble you got into Sadday night."

"I don't want to stay out there no longer." Cleveland still had not taken the chair that Bully offered. He continued to stand at the doorway, looking in toward the bed where Daly was talking to Ruby Lee. "I can't stay there, Papa. I come back here to stay and farm with you."

"Mr. John goin' to come lookin' for you," Bully said. "You know the white man goin' to be here lookin' for you."

"He don't need to find me," Cleveland said. "I don't need to be at the house when the white man come. Ruby Lee don't need to be here."

Daly came to the porch again. "You can't stay, Cleveland. We don't want no trouble with Mr. John."

Cleveland looked from one of them to the other. He swung his head slowly as he looked at his mother and his father. "I done come home," he said. "I done come back to be with you-all. What else I'm goin' to do? Where else I'm goin' to go?"

"You better go back to the man," Bully said. "You better go back and work out what you owe to the man."

"What about Ruby Lee? What if he come back there when she at the house by herself? I work here with you, Papa. I farm with you and pay the man when we make a crop in the fall."

"Lawd, ha' mercy," said Daly. "Jesus God."

"We can't do that, Clevelan'." Bully sounded weary. His shoulders sagged, his head was bent, and even in the darkness he could not look straight at Cleveland. "Us ain't goin' to make no crop this year. Us ain't goin' to make no more crop on this place."

"I still got the mules," Cleveland said. "I left the mules in the lot and I go back and get them and bring them out here."

Bully shook his head. "Us ain't goin' to use them mules here," he said. "Us don't own the place now. Mr. John done bought the place and made the papers on it. We done made the deal; us goin' to move next month. Us can't farm the place, Clevelan', it don't belong to us."

CHAPTER TWENTY-TWO

Cleveland did not have time to let Bully's words sink in before he jerked his head up and stared through the darkness toward the bend of the road as it came up from Spring Creek. The words were hanging there without his fully understanding them when he stopped listening to Bully and started listening to a sound that came on the south wind from the direction of the creek. Twin streaks of light cut above the treetops; then suddenly the streaks leveled, and across the road from the house the trees jumped like tall, waiting sentries into sharp relief as the light struck them and held them detached from the shadowed woods.

"That's Mr. John. I know that motor. Lawd God, I know the sound of that truck." Cleveland backed toward the door while he kept his eyes on the approaching lights. "He comin' here. He comin' to look for me. Talk to him, Papa," Cleveland said. "Talk to him and keep him in the yard."

He stepped inside the room, but Ruby Lee was out of the bed moving ahead of him. Her feet were quick as she crossed the floor to the kitchen, and the light there dimmed and went out as she turned down the lampwick and puffed across the chimney. Cleveland backed across the room through the darkness, still looking out the door toward the brightly lighted trees across the road where the headlights swept an arc as the truck rounded the curve at the top of the hill.

Hoodoo and Little Suster came out of the side room. Little Suster was rubbing at her eyes with her hand, and Hoodoo yawned. He had on a white undershirt of Bully's that came down almost to his knees. Little Suster had on a nightshirt that Daly had made for her.

"Papa," Hoodoo said, "what the matter? Who that talkin' out here?"

"Get back in the room, Hoodoo," Cleveland said fiercely. "Get back in the room and keep yo' mouth closed or I knock you in the head."

"Clevelan'!" Little Suster shrieked. "What you doin'? When you come?"

"Keep quiet," Cleveland snapped. "You-all get in the room and stay quiet or I bust yo' heads."

"Go back in the room," Ruby Lee whispered from the kitchen door. "Stay in there and don't talk and don't holler to Clevelan'."

The brakes squeaked shrilly as the truck stopped in front of the yard gate. The motor died and the lights went out.

Cleveland edged toward the corner of the room between

the kitchen door and the fireplace. The shotgun stood there. Bully kept the shotgun standing there. It would be unloaded because of the children. Cleveland edged toward the mantel and started feeling along it, feeling with his hand for the cardboard box of shells.

The truck door slammed and John Chaney's voice called "Hello" from the side of the road.

"Good e'nin'," Bully answered from the porch. "Who there?"

"You know God-damn' well who it is, Bully," the white man said, rattling at the fence. "How do you open this gate?"

"Pull out on it, Mr. John," Bully said. "Pull on it and lift it up a little and it open."

Bully stood on the porch to one side of the door. Daly stood close by him. The white man would come from the gate straight to the steps. Cleveland felt with his hand for the shells.

"Don't, Clevelan'!" Ruby Lee whispered hoarsely. She was closer than he thought and she had seen him glance toward the corner as she went to blow out the light. "Clevelan', don't do that."

He felt her grab his arm as it was raised to let him feel along the mantel. She grabbed it so hard she knocked his wrist against the edge of the wood. He felt a quick twinge of pain where the muscle and the bone grated together as she dragged down on his arm. "Don't, Clevelan'!"

He swung his arm to throw her back, but she hung on tight; she dragged herself up close to him, still whispering. "Don't do that, Clevelan'. Lea' the man alone."

"Where's Cleveland?" John Chaney asked from the foot of the steps. "I'm lookin' for that boy, Bully. I been out to the bottoms this evening and they told me he left again."

"Cleveland ain't done nothin', Mr. John? He ain't been in no meanness?" It was Daly asking.

"Where is he, Bully? I know that boy's here." John Chaney's voice was high and thin; it broke a little when the white man was angry, and made him sound as though he were out of breath.

Cleveland could not get his arm loose to reach into the corner. Ruby Lee hung onto him. She held him so that he could hardly move. "It wouldn't do no good, Clevelan'," she whispered. "Don't cause no more trouble with the white man." He did not know she was so strong. Her fingers were digging into his arm. "The baby yours, Clevelan'. Don't cause no trouble now. It won't do no good. I go back with you to the bottoms."

"Cleveland owes me money," John Chaney said. "He's run off and left me in the middle of makin' that crop. He can't do that, Bully—he knows he can't do that."

Cleveland struggled with her, trying to get loose, but she hung on. Their feet scraped on the floor, Ruby Lee's bare feet making a soft sound on the planks, Cleveland's shoes scraping and bumping. She wouldn't let go, and then suddenly Cleveland felt the burning fuse of his anger die out.

He felt his feet heavy, his legs tired. He felt the weariness that filled his body rise up again to cloud the sharp plan of his movements—the corner, the gun, and the shells. He felt tired, tired. "I'll go," he said low under his breath. He shook his arm, and Ruby Lee let go of it. His feet dragged as he walked toward the door; his shoe heels sounded hollow against the boards.

"Here I am, Mr. John," Cleveland said. He could barely see the white man standing there in the yard, but he spoke toward John Chaney's shape. "I had to come home. My wife been sick."

"I'll take you back to jail, Cleveland," John Chaney said. "You run away while you was out on bond, and you know I can have you put in jail for that."

"I goin' back in the mornin', Mr. John," Cleveland said. "I left them mules in the lot. They got to be fed and watered in the mornin'."

"Be God-damned if you're goin' to run off and leave me

while I got a crop to make," John Chaney said. "Cleveland, you know better than that."

"I had to leave, Mr. John. My wife sick."

"Ruby Lee been po'ly, Mr. John," Daly said. "She ain't been feelin' well."

"I be back in the mornin'," Cleveland said. "I had to come out here today."

"If you're lying to me I'll send the sheriff after you, Cleveland. You God-damn' people are ungrateful. I get you out of jail Monday morning and you run off and leave me Wednesday evening. You better be back, Cleveland."

"He be back, Mr. John," Bully told the white man. "He stay here tonight and rest, but I see that he start early in the mornin'. He be back there before dinnertime tomorrow."

John Chaney stood there a moment longer, but he had nothing more to say. In the dark they could barely make him out as he turned. The yard gate squeaked behind him and the truck door slammed. The lights came on and the white man started his motor and pulled ten yards up the road to where the gap for the wagon was cut. He turned in, backed out, sawed across the road twice, and then was straightened out toward town. The truck lights punched at the trees banked beyond the curve at the top of the hill, and then he was gone.

The night grew darker yet while the earth turned slowly and the sun sank deeper and deeper beneath the western horizon. A thin moon that did nothing to lighten the shadows underneath the trees along the road or to touch the road itself with a glow of its own broke for a moment from behind scudding clouds driven by the south wind and then disappeared again, dipping toward the woods beyond the river. In the side room Unca Dempse lay in his bed asleep, never wakened by the talk at the front of the house. Hoodoo and Little Suster had gone back to sleep on their pallets, and if Vincent on his cot against the wall and Tina on her pallet in the front room had wakened, then they had kept still and wondered, for there had been no word from them.

The front room was quiet now. Daly was asleep, and Bully lay beside her in the bed. Ruby Lee lay on a folded quilt near Tina's pallet. Whether or not she slept Cleveland did not know, but she was quiet, she was not stirring. And still Cleveland found no rest. He was tired all over, his body weary and sore, his feet hurting from the long walk on hard roads. But still he could not rest.

He sat on the edge of the porch and propped his back against a roof post. He rolled and smoked his cigarettes, and the damp wind made the fiery end glow, lighting up the dark planes of his face in the night.

Well, it looked like every way he turned . . . Well, Bully had sold the place. Well, he walked all evening to get off the white man's land and it was still underneath his feet. It ran through his head like a song:

Well, well—well—well—
Well, Long John,
He's long gone. . . .

Little Suster's tomcat came around the corner of the house and jumped up on the porch. Stopping suddenly, the cat arched his back and swelled his tail while he looked at Cleveland, surprised by the figure at the edge of the porch. "Hey, cat," Cleveland said softly. He stretched out his hand and scratched the floor. "Hey, cat." The big tomcat whirled, hissing, and his claws dug up the floor as he shot back over the edge to the ground. He was gone.

Cleveland dragged deep at the end of his cigarette. He flipped the butt as far as he could in the darkness. The glowing end made a red arc in the night and showered sparks as it hit the yard fence. Cleveland let his breath out; he could barely see the smoke as it jetted from his nostrils and was caught up by the quiet wind and carried away, separating, spreading, thinning, become nothing in the damp air that moved through the trees and blew across the river and the fields.

CHAPTER TWENTY-THREE

The hind wheels of the truck were down in a little ditch by the side of the road. The front wheels rested on the roadbed, and the tail gate was down, swinging above the ground in front of the low gate that opened out of Bully Webster's yard. "Get up in the truck, Walter," Bully said, "and I lift the bed up to you." Bully's arms were thick and his shoulders strong, but he was a little stooped. He had no hat on and his forehead was slightly beaded with sweat in the morning sunlight. He had his denim jumper on over blue overalls. His hands were dark on the back, and the lighter palms were work-roughened. His fingers were knobbed and crooked, but strong as they grasped the head part of an iron bedstead and lifted it up so that one leg rested on the floor of the truck.

"Shove it on," Walter Steptoe said. "I got it." The broken roller on the leg of the frame scraped across the wooden floor of the truck bed. Muscles bulged in his broad back as Walter stooped to lift the frame forward and lean it against the side of the stake body.

"Carry it all the way up there," Bully told him. "Stack it tight. Us got to get all them things loaded on here and just make one trip."

"We get it on here, all right," Walter Steptoe said. "They plenty of room in this truck to hold it all."

On the porch of the house behind them Bully's children came out to hear the talk and look at the truck pulled up in front of the yard. Vincent was already there, picking up a loaded box to carry to the truck, and Tina came out of the door behind Hoodoo and Little Suster. The porch around them was covered with gear moved from the inside of the house. There were the railings and the slats and the footboard that Bully and Walter had left when they carried the head frame out to the road. There were the broken box springs and the mattress and a small stack of folded quilts. There was a wooden box filled with a couple of frying pans, a Dutch oven, stewpans, and an aluminum kettle. A big iron washpot had been rolled around to lean against the edge of the porch.

Daly came to the door of the house to look over Tina's shoulder. She held a broom in her hands and had a stocking cap pulled over her hair. Her sleeves were rolled up over strong brown arms, and her eyes moved quickly, sharply, as she surveyed the work at the front of the house. But her face was tired and anxious when she leaned her broom against the door and lifted her apron to wipe perspiration from her forehead.

"Hoodoo," she snapped, seeing the boy settling down on the pile of quilts. "Hoodoo, you come off that porch and get out to the barn to catch them chickens. You better move on, boy, and get them chickens caught."

Two hens lay quietly at the far edge of the porch, their legs tied together with torn strips of cloth. Another hen ran loose in the yard. She was Daly's pet hen, a frizzly chicken with her feathers fuzzed up on her neck and body as if she had got too close to a fire and singed herself, curling up all her feathers.

Little Suster jumped down from the edge of the porch and tried to catch the hen, but the chicken squawked and flew, heading around the corner of the house toward the back yard. Little Suster ran after her, yelling for Hoodoo to head her off.

"Don't you run them chickens," Daly shouted. "Hoodoo, you shell some corn and catch them chickens in the lot."

There was a breeze blowing, but the heat given off by the August sun as it rose higher grew stronger and began to make the smooth, grassless expanse of dirt yard warm underfoot. Walter Steptoe carried the washpot to the truck, and Vincent followed him with the box full of cooking pans. Bully stacked the bed slats and shouldered them. His shoes stirred the dirt of the yard into faint dust as he walked the already distinguishable path to the back end of the truck.

Unca Dempse came from inside the house as Bully and Vincent returned to the porch for another load. "Where my tobacco can?" the old man asked. "Where you-all put my can of tobacco?" He walked with a cane, which he lifted and used as a stick to poke at the pile of folded quilts as he paused and peered the length of the cluttered porch. "My pipe done gone out," he said. "If them chillun done losed that can I be plumb without tobacco. I whup them chillun with this stick if they done losed that can."

"Yo' tobacco in here on the shelf, Papa," Daly called from inside the house. "Yo' tobacco in here where you left it. Ain't nobody touched it." She came out to the porch and put down a box of dishes.

"You-all be careful with them plates," she told Bully. "That's all we got. You break them plates and I don't know what we goin' to eat off of." She looked toward the growing pile in the truck and then at the still heaped porch.

"That's just about all they is inside the house," she said. "If them chillun get them chickens caught and get on back here we get it pretty well cleaned out. It all goin' to get on the truck?" She looked again to see how much room there was.

Walter Steptoe laughed. "That truck haul two bales of cotton at one time," he said. "And then you don't have to tromp it none. We get all yo' stuff on." He lifted two straight-backed, rawhide-bottomed chairs, picking them up in his huge hands as if they were toys, and went across the yard again.

Walter stood up straight and looked down the road as he got into the truck. "Yonder come the man," he called. "Mr. John comin' around the curve yonder above Spring Creek."

The sound of John Chaney's pickup came ahead of it down the road. In a moment, from the house they could see the thin film of white dust that rose behind the truck and spread out among the trees on either side of the road.

The pickup slowed and pulled around the front of the truck that stood before the gate, coming to a stop at the edge of the ditch at the far corner of the yard. John Chaney stepped down, and the door slammed behind him as he walked back to the side of the big truck.

"You gettin' started early," the white man said.

"Yassuh," Bully agreed. "We want to get down while it's still cool. We ain't got too much to put on here. I reckon we get in there and get unloaded before this e'nin'."

Unca Dempse saw John Chaney move to stand by the yard fence. The old man left the porch and shuffled across the yard. "How you, Mr. John?" he asked. "How you this mornin'?"

"All right, Unca Dempse. They been makin' you work to carry that stuff out on the porch?"

The old man shook his head. "They done all that," he said. "They done moved all them things. I didn't do none of it." He looked up at the white man standing there on the other side of the fence. "I don't much want to move, Mr. John," he said. "I been in this one place too long to want to leave it."

"You been here a long time," John Chaney said. "I been tryin' to talk Bully into stayin' and farmin' it for me. I don't know why he won't listen to me."

"Us been had this place," Unca Dempse went on, not paying much attention to what the white man said. "My granddaddy had this place give to him when slavery times was over. Mr. Will Dawson give my granddaddy this land at the end of the war. Us been had this place ever since."

John Chaney was becoming impatient while the old man talked. He shoved his hat back on his head and mopped at his face with the white handkerchief. "I know that, Unca Dempse," he said again. "You been a good neighbor to me long as I've had that place up the river."

"The land pretty good, Mr. John," Unca Dempse said. "The land all right, but us can't fight the river. I don't blame Bully none for sayin' we got to move. The water done got us. The water don't let us make no crop. I don't want to leave the land," he said, turning to watch Bully and Vincent lifting a chest of drawers up to Walter Steptoe, "but I too old now. I too old to keep on fightin' the river."

"Papa," Daly called from the porch, "here yo' tobacco. You talk Mr. John to death out there if you don't watch out."

The old man grunted, shifting his head as he listened to Daly. He turned slowly toward the house and leaned on his cane as he raised his glance to peer across the yard toward the door and the porch litter. Indignant, he said, "Keep the tobacco. I don't need it now." He needed no stick for walking, since he still could stand straight when he reminded himself of it. He carried himself erect, but used the cane to give him steadiness when he climbed the steps or when he was getting up from a chair. He was of the same light color that showed in Daly's skin, and his face was strong beneath the lines that marked it. It was only when he was drinking his milk from a glass that his jaw wobbled and his hands shook. When he held his pipe clinched between his teeth his jaw was firm. His feet shuffled when he walked, but his path was straight. He left the white man standing there by the fence to circle the house and go toward the barn, and they heard him shouting from there, "Hoodoo! Hoodoo, don't you run them chickens. You shell that corn and throw it on the ground and toll them up to you."

The white man lit a cigarette and drew on it while he stood by the yard fence. His tallness was accentuated by the short palings. The foot that he propped on the fence was encased in a dusty, red-stained cowboy boot. His straw hat, broad-brimmed and pinch-crowned, was showing dirt smudges on the bent brim in front. Though the sun was at his back and the hat threw a shade, his face showed glowing red, as if it were reflecting the fire on the end of his cigarette. He was leaning over to rest an elbow on the knee that was propped high, and the bending made his belt crease his stomach. His blue eyes were pale and indistinct above the red of his cheeks, and his voice was exceptionally high and thin—like it was too early in the morning and he had not yet been able to clear his throat. His hand was nervous, moving quickly as it put the cigarette to his lips while he took a short puff, then jerking away as if the paper burned when it touched.

"I wish you would stay on, Bully," he said. "I'd like for you to stay on the place. You're a good hand, and I'd like to keep you here. With a good team you could make a crop."

"We done got the place rented in town, Mr. John," Bully said, wiping at his forehead as he spoke. "I reckon we let the farmin' go for a while. I thought you was goin' to move Clevelan' out here."

The white man grunted, dragging at his smoke. "I'm through fooling with trying to get him to farm a place. I can't depend on him to make a crop for me. It looks like going back to day labor will suit him better." Straightening, taking his foot off the fence, Chaney dismissed the thought of Cleveland. "Then what are you goin' to do, Bully? You got anything to do in town?"

"I supposed to go to the oil mill next week," Bully answered. "I supposed to start workin' there Monday in the seed house."

"That work is too heavy for a man as old as you, Bully," John Chaney said. "I wish you'd decide to stay on here and farm this place for me."

Bully laughed a little as he shook his head. "Nawsuh, Mr. John. We done sold you the place, and I reckon we better move. We make out in town; I find enough to do for us to make out."

He looked at the white man standing at the side of the road. He wondered howcome Mr. John thought he would stay there when Cleveland, much as the boy had wanted to come back to the place, would not have it now. He wondered how the white man figured he would stay and farm the place. It was too late now; he was through with it. The land was gone. It belonged to Mr. John, and if the white man wanted somebody to farm it he would have to move another man out there. He'd have to get somebody else to fight the weeds and the grass and wait for the water to come up out of the river and flood over the crops. He'd have to let somebody else take a team and work that thick black land in the bottoms where the Johnson grass roots went deep into the soil, where the bloodweeds grew tall along the turnrows and the brown cottonstalks rotted in the earth.

"We done got a place to live in town, Mr. John," Bully said. "I reckon we stay there a while."

Hoodoo and Little Suster stood in the middle of the barn lot while the chickens pecked at the grains of corn scattered on the ground about them. There were five hens and one rooster left. "Them chickens gettin' wild," Hoodoo said. "Ease up on the red hen, Little Suster, while I throw down some more corn."

He shelled more grains from the ear held in his hand and dropped them close around their feet. The red hen pecked closer, and Little Suster stooped and made a grab for her. The red hen squawked and flapped her wings, but she was caught by the legs. Little Suster moved toward the fence while the rest of the chickens ran off and then stopped to look before coming back to slip up on a grain of corn, dart at it, and then run away again.

"They goin' to have to quieten down before we catch another one," Hoodoo said, taking a strip of rag from his pocket. "Hold her foots while I tie them together." He tied a knot about one of the chicken's legs, then pulled the other close and knotted it also, and Little Suster put the red hen in the coop that stood near the lot gap.

"I wish us didn't have to move," Little Suster said. "I don't know whether I like stayin' in town all the time. I just as soon stay out here and go to town on Sadday."

"I rather stay in town," Hoodoo said, shelling a handful of corn. "Ain't no cotton to pick. I rather stay in town and get me a job at the oil mill with Papa than work in the field all day."

"You ain't picked no cotton this year," Little Suster told him. "Ain't been no cotton for you to pick."

Hoodoo threw the corn toward the chickens. "I don't aim to pick no cotton. I'm through with the field. I'm goin' to go to work with Papa."

"Papa say us goin' back to school. He say us goin' to the school in town."

"I ain't goin' to no school. I ain't studyin' goin' to town to go to no school."

"Papa say us goin'." Little Suster kicked the back of her heels against the coop and set the chickens inside to fluttering. Her eyes gleamed when she turned her head to look at Hoodoo. When she teased him it made him stick out his under lip.

"I wish you quit talkin'," Hoodoo grunted. "I wish you get up and help me catch these chickens." He made a grab for a hen that walked close in front of them. He missed and the hen flew. Hoodoo started after her, running around the barn lot, and the chickens were scared again.

Out in front of the house the truck was filling up. The heavy things were all in, and now there were the bedclothes and the rest of the chairs and the table to finish off the load.

John Chaney was still out there by the truck, watching how they put the furniture and the clothes in on top of the bed-frames and the cookstove and the iron washpot. "Not goin' to take you much longer, is it, Bully?" he asked in his high voice.

"We soon have it all," Bully said. "We just about through." With his thumbnail he dug at a small splinter in the palm of his hand and turned toward the white man. "I'm sho' glad you sent this truck to move us, Mr. John. Without no team I don't know how else we would have got us things in to town."

"You're lucky to get this truck today," John Chaney said. "My cotton is beginning to open pretty fast now, and I've got pickers in the field tryin' to get that cotton out before the rains get to it." He turned his head slightly. "You're goin' to have to get on out there to the bottoms soon as you get Bully unloaded, Walter. Maybe you'll have time to haul a bale in before you get ready to take the pickers home."

"I don't know what we would have done without this truck," Bully said.

"It was in the deal I made with you," John Chaney replied. "But you caught me at a short time; that's why I say you're lucky I could send this truck out here."

The white man kept standing around out there while they were loading the truck, and Bully could not understand it. He wasn't going to carry off anything that didn't belong to him. He had made his deal with Mr. John and sold him the place, and now he was getting off it. The white man didn't have to come out there and watch him while he moved. The white man was getting the land cheap. He was getting the land for twenty dollars an acre; what else did he want? Only thing the white man threw in for boot was the truck to carry them away.

"Twenty dollars, Bully," the white man had said. "That's all it's worth. What good is the land goin' to do me when it's six feet under water? What can I do with the land then?"

John Chaney got another cigarette lit and shook the match in his hand to kill the flame. "You ought to save some of that money, Bully," he said. "You know that when you niggers get hold of money it's gone. Why don't you put away some of that money I paid you and have somethin' for yourself when you need it?"

"I wish I could save some," Bully answered. "I wish I could save enough to get goin' again. I rather work for myself, Mr. John; I rather try to make a livin' for myself in these bottoms along this river than take a job there in town where I got all sorts of men tellin' me what to do."

"I know," John Chaney said. "That's the kind you are.

You're a good man, Bully, but you're too God-damn' independent. I'd like to have you stay on this place and work it for me."

"I reckon not, Mr. John. I wouldn't want to stay on the place and it not be ours."

The white man did not like that too well—Bully could see it in his face. He wanted somebody to work the place; he had wanted to move Cleveland out there, but Cleveland had shook his head and said, "Nawsuh, Mr. John, I work for you here. I pick cotton for you this fall and pay off what I owe, but I don't want to go back out yonder," and the white man was tired of fooling with a contrary nigger like that. Lacking Cleveland, he had wanted Bully to stay on and work the place, because Bully knew the land and Bully was a good farmer. But now here was Bully acting just as Cleveland had.

Mr. John was puffing on the butt of his cigarette, making the fire end of it glow brightly even in the sunshine. His face was red under the brim of his hat. There was a breeze blowing, but it looked as if the morning were too hot for him.

He threw the end of his cigarette down and stood up straight. "You-all can get started when you finish loading," he said. "You needn't wait for me, Walter. I'm goin' to walk down toward the river and look around the place."

"Yassuh, Mr. John," Walter Steptoe said. He and Bully stood still to watch the white man go down the road a few yards, step over the fence, and walk across the pasture that came up to the barn lot.

"He goin' to walk all over this place," Walter Steptoe said from where he stood at the very back end of the loaded truck bed. "That man sho' do like to walk around and look at his land."

"He ain't goin' to see much but dried cornstalks and bloodweeds," Bully said. "Down there along the river he might see some yaupon thickets. The land rich, all right, but he ain't goin' to see no crop on it."

"Well, that's about all they is," Bully said. They had the bedclothes on, and the chicken coop was tied to the back of the load. The truck bed was full, and the house was cleaned out. The barn lot stood empty and deserted. The hard, packed dirt of the yard was marked with a path where they had crossed it carrying load after load of furniture and clothes. The fire was out, no smoke came out of the chimney, and already the house looked as vacant as if it had been standing empty there for years.

"Well, now, I reckon we about ready to go," Bully said. The air was still and the sun shone brightly. The breeze that had blown earlier was almost gone. The land lay quiet. The road was deserted except for John Chaney's pickup and the big truck that was backed up to Bully's front yard gate with its bed piled high. The sun that had made Bully and Walter Steptoe and Vincent take off their jumpers while they were loading the truck touched the feathers of a flying crow and burnished them gleaming purple as the crow veered away to circle around the house and the trucks that stood before it.

The land lay still. Who could tell that it had been plowed? Who could tell where the plows had run and furrowed the earth? Where the waters came the land was flat. The waters leveled everything—smoothed out the furrows, melted the clods, and silted over the turnrows. After the waters came how could you tell that a man had scratched the ground and sweated over it and worn himself down working with it? Because the land was rich it gave food to the weeds and the vines just as quick as it did to the cotton and the corn and the peas and the sugar cane. The richness was there to make a crop, but the weeds and the grass lived off the richness too. The earth did not care. All roots were alike. The red water of the river was the lifeblood of the land, but it was the death also, for what the river gave it took away.

"Daly, why don't you and Unca Dempse ride in the cab with Walter?" Bully asked. "Me and the chillun ride on the load and keep things from fallin' off."

Maybe the bones of the Beck mule were still down there in the pasture, bleached and white, scattered by the buzzards and the roving dogs. Maybe the bones of that bobtailed, black-faced muley cow lay somewhere along the river bank, buried under the mud. But they would not be there after the river rose and changed the mudbanks again. Bully was leaving the land as he found it—gone to weeds and grass, gone to tie vines and briers.

If the white man put the land in pasture it would go back to the river. The grass would take all the rich bottom land, and the yaupon thickets would begin to creep out from the bank of the river. If the white man farmed it he could keep it clean. He had money enough and gear enough to farm it and take what the river would let him have. It was a gamble all around, but the white man could afford to take the chance. One good crop made on the land would pay him for two lost. Bully could not farm it that way. The river had the upper hand, the river held the balance, and how could you fight the river when you did not have any mule at all?

"Us goin' to town," Hoodoo said. "Us goin' to live in town."

Hoodoo had it right; the circle was complete. Bully had come out here and now he was going back, and who could tell the difference? He did not even have "Bully Webster" cut into a sycamore tree to show that he had been there, as he had cut when he was a boy on Mr. Wallace Bryan's place on the Brazos. The land lay smooth. Nobody could tell where his plow had been, nobody could see a mark he had left—and say that here he tried to make it and didn't.

Tina and Vincent already were settled into comfortable seats on the piled quilts when Little Suster scrambled up to the top of the load on the truck. Little Suster was trying to find a place to rest her feet when she looked toward the house again. "Yonder my cat," she screamed. "Lawd, I done forgot my cat. Wait up, Papa, while I gets my cat."

"Hold on, Walter," Bully shouted, and Walter leaned over to look out of the cab window.

Little Suster climbed down to the yard again. She ran to the porch and called to the cat. The big tom looked at her and walked away. Hoodoo had been pestering him too much; he was not ready to be friendly with anybody. Little Suster grabbed for the cat and the cat ran. He crossed the porch and jumped to the ground, then turned under the house to look out again.

"Lea' the cat alone, Little Suster," Bully called. "Come on back here. Us got to get started."

"I want to take my cat," Little Suster said. She was almost crying.

"We ain't got time to wait while you chase that cat," Bully said. "Let him go, he wild anyhow; that cat wouldn't do no good in town. Come back here, Little Suster."

She came across the yard, her bare feet padding the dirt. Tears stood in her eyes while she climbed up on the truck again.

Walter turned the key in the switch and stepped on the starter. The motor whined as he fed it gas, and the truck bed groaned as it slowly rocked up out of the shallow ditch and straightened out on the road toward town.

The cat would make out in the woods. He was already fat from catching and eating field larks. That cat would catch him a rat or a salamander without any trouble. Let the cat go, he belonged to stay on the place. He was afraid of the water; he wouldn't go near the river. The cat would make out all right.

The truck pulled away down the road, and the place was left behind them with John Chaney's pickup standing in front of the house. They turned the curve and went down the hill to cross Spring Creek with Walter driving slowly so nothing would be bounced off the load. The white dust rose up in a cloud behind them after they had crossed the creek and started the pull out of the bottom land.

About halfway to town Bully looked back and saw John Chaney driving after them. The white man was coming on fast in the pickup. He came up behind them and pulled around the truck, never slowing, and the dust kicked up by his passing clouded the air and caught on their hair as they rode through it.

CHAPTER TWENTY-FOUR

The boll weevil is a little black bug,
Come from Mexico, they say;
Come all the way to Texas
Just lookin' for a place to stay.
Just lookin' for a home,
Just lookin' for a home.

That white dog of Joe Coby's must not have had good sense. He ought to have known better than to run out and bark at people on the road at night; it looked like he would learn sometime that he was going to get in trouble if he kept on running out to snap and growl at a man's heels. There might be some reason for him to bark when there was somebody passing in front of the house or sneaking around the yard or the barn lot, but out on the open road in the big middle of the bottoms that dog didn't have a reason in the world to come running out of the cotton to bark at a man.

The dog ought to tend to his own business. He had jumped a rabbit at the edge of the field and run him through the cotton until the rabbit was clean gone, but if the dog had tended to his business and stayed in the field he might have jumped the rabbit again down by the creek bank. The white dog was hungry, and the running and yipping after the rabbit had left him panting and thirsty, but that gave him no right to come bursting out of the cotton to bark at Cleveland like he did.

The dog was a long way from Joe Coby's house, a long way removed from the place he might have had some right to protect by barking. But ever since Joe had moved off to the Navasot' and left the place the dog had not hung around there much. Joe had been gone two days now, and the dog just came to the house to lie under the porch during the heat of the day. Joe had tried to take the dog with him. After the truck was loaded he tried to catch the white dog and get him into the cab. But the dog didn't like trucks; he didn't like the sound of the motor and the smell of burning oil. He howled and set his feet, and Joe had to drag him along by the scruff of the neck, and when Joe lifted him into the cab the dog gave one wild scratching flounce and shot out of the window, leaving blood on Joe's arm where the hind claws had dug into the flesh. Joe decided to come back later and get the dog.

Since then the white dog had prowled around looking for something to eat. There was plenty of water in the creek for him to drink, but he had a harder time finding meat. He would go around to the back door of the house around noontime, but there was nothing there for him. And in the evening when the air cooled and the dirt between the rows of cotton was not so burning hot to the pads of his feet, the dog would nose out to try to jump some swamp rabbit or cottontail that had strayed away from the brush along the creek. The dog was not fast; he was too lazy from lying around the house all summer eating table scraps. He had caught only one rabbit, a young one, and that was early in the morning of the day before. The rabbit tonight was an old one, quick and smart, and the dog had lost it before they crossed twenty rows of cotton.

But it was no matter if the dog was hungry and thirsty—that didn't make it right for him to come out barking and growling just because there was a man walking the road in the dark.

Cleveland had a big sack of groceries cradled in his right arm. He shifted the sack when he heard the dog, and his hand dropped to his side to touch the pocket where his knife lay. "That God-damn' dog again," Cleveland said. "He goin' to fool around with me once too often."

It was late, and Cleveland was in a hurry to get back from the store. He had to walk nearly all the way to the highway before he would get to Book Turner's house, and he was hungry. It was past his suppertime. He had gone to the store after he left the field in the evening, because it was too far up there, and the weather was still too warm for Ruby Lee to be going after groceries. She was carrying that baby; she couldn't carry a sack too. There was plenty to eat in the house; Book could have got groceries for Cleveland and Ruby Lee, but Cleveland would not see it that way. He would live with Ruby Lee's folks while she was having the baby, that was all right. But he was going to eat his own rations.

He was tired. He was in a hurry to get back to the house, and there that white dog came, raising hell. Cleveland turned, and the dog stopped. "You better get on; you better leave out from here." The dog snuffled. His white fur made him stand out against the dark background of the road and the field of opening cotton. He flopped his tongue to the inside of his mouth and whined; his tail drooped. Cleveland took a lunging step toward the dog, making noises. "Hanh! Get on!" But the white dog dropped to his belly in the dirt and whined again, looking up to see what the man was going to do next.

Cleveland waited, and the dog lay there. Then Cleveland sucked air through his lips, and the dog inched forward in the dust. Cleveland bent over until his hand touched the slick, short-haired head. The dog whined, his tongue coming out again to run over his nose and his chops and then hang panting, dripping saliva. "Hey dog," Cleveland said. "Hey, dog."

Cleveland headed down the road again. His feet in their cut-open shoes made little noise in the dust that lay thick and heavy on the turnrow road. The paper sack rustled in his arms as he shifted it from one side to the other to make his load ride easy. Joe Coby's white dog fell in behind and followed Cleveland all the way to Book Turner's house, followed at a slow trot with his feet silent in the dust, with his head low and his tongue panting, hanging and dripping.

AFTERWORD

High John the Conqueror is a remarkable novel, and yet it is as simple and down to earth as a genre painting. The novel is remarkable partly because it was decades ahead of its time in treating race relations in Texas; partly because the sexual harassment theme prefigures the late-century emphasis on sexual politics; and partly because the novel's picture of the small farmer's unhappy lot does not suffer by comparison with such farm-life classics as Steinbeck's *The Grapes of Wrath* (1939) or Texan George Sessions Perry's *Hold Autumn in Your Hand* (1941).

There were few novels being published in America in 1948 that treated African Americans as sensitive human beings, and I know of no Texas novel written before 1950 that speaks so strongly against racism as *High John* does. Before Wilson's novel appeared, Negroes in Texas fiction were almost always depicted as comic characters of the Step-and-Fetchit sort or as loyal, simple-minded servants. Molly Moore Davis' 1895 novel *Under the Man-Fig*, Laura Krey's 1938 bestseller *And Tell of Time*, and Elizabeth Lee Wheaton's *Mr. George's Joint* (1941) are all cases in point. But with John W. Wilson's novel, we see blacks who live and breathe and suffer the same "slings and arrows" as humans always have.

High John the Conqueror is relevant to life in our time not only for its emphasis on the questions of race and sex; but for its depiction of the perilous nature of the family farm as the nation turned to giant agribusiness; and for its depiction of the almost intolerable lives of the underclasses.

Many of the problems that small farmers faced in the years just before World War II, they face today – those few who are still left on the land in this era of factory farms. Because agribusiness has more access to bank loans, more money for equipment, more ability to resist natural disaster, it has largely replaced the small farmer that Thomas Jefferson saw as the backbone of American culture.

Like many small farmers of the past and present, Bully Webster and his family held on as long as they could to the forty acres which had been under black ownership since the Civil War. But by the novel's end, the future is clear for the poor black family: they must sell out to John Chaney for twenty dollars an acre and move into the town of Navasota. As the tale of an American farmer of the twentieth century, Bully Webster's story could be about whites as well as about blacks. (Texas writer John Cherry Watson's *The Red Dress*, which came out a year after *High John*, follows the fortunes of white families who are forced off their farms near Smithville – not far from Navasota.) What Bully and his family have to do is what millions of small farmers have done in this century when times got impossible: they move to town and join the urban underclass. Given the chance to sharecrop on land that now belongs to John Chaney, Bully refuses by telling Chaney, "we done got the place rented in town. . . . I reckon we let the farmin' go for awhile."

Before the book opens, Bully and his wife Daly, like the

farmers in European folktales, have had to send one of their children–Cleveland, the strongest and most reliable–out to make his own way in life. The farm won't support Unca Dempse, his daughter Daly and son-in-law Bully, and all their children. So Cleveland, who has recently married Ruby Lee Turner, has become a day laborer and later a sharecropper on one of John Chaney's many farms. While Bully sees his farm slipping away, Cleveland, working for Chaney, is doing as well as tenant farmers ever do. But he is constantly beset with jealousy because John Chaney, the "High John" of the title, has begun to drop by and visit Ruby Lee when Cleveland is not at home. Or he will visit Cleveland as a pretext for looking at Ruby Lee. Ruby Lee is afraid not to be polite to the white man, and that puts further suspicions in Cleveland's mind.

When Ruby Lee becomes pregnant, Cleveland doubts that the child she is carrying is his. But like Ruby Lee, Cleveland dreads confrontation with John Chaney, a man of considerable power in that country where the Navasota River runs into the Brazos. (In the novel, the characters always speak of the river as "the Navasot," a short form used by whites and blacks who live in the rich bottom lands of the lower Brazos.) John Chaney's power over Ruby Lee is the essence of sexual harassment. Even though we are privy to no scenes where he forces himself on her, the power of the large white plantation owner terrifies her–and enrages Cleveland. Chaney is not successful in his pursuit of Ruby Lee, but that doesn't alter the fact that he is guilty. In today's world, men have been prosecuted for doing no more than Chaney does. Added to his power as a rich farmer is the fact of his whiteness in a Jim Crow world. Neither Cleveland nor Buddy Boy can afford to act insulted when John Chaney berates them for fighting in the field by saying: "What the hell are you black sons of bitches tryin' to do?" And when Cleveland is arrested in the town of Navasota for drunkenness and for carrying a switchblade, the sheriff matter-of-factly says, "Mr. John asked me to take care of his niggers tonight." In late-thirties Texas, a white man could call the men "black sons of bitches" and prey on a black woman with relative impunity. The husband of an African American woman knew the danger of confronting a white man who set out in pursuit of his wife.

The main theme that runs through *High John the Conqueror* is the uncertain life of the small farmer. As far back as the eighteenth century, the precarious nature of the small farmer was a theme of literature. Goldsmith's "The Deserted Village" shows life in "Sweet Auburn, loveliest village of the plain" after the industrial revolution has begun draining the countryside of cottage workers and small farmers. And though the family farm remained the agricultural paradigm of American life until late in the nineteenth century—and until this day is the bucolic ideal for most Americans—the demise of the small farmer was evident early in the twentieth century. Today's "Farm Aid Concerts" and unrealistic price-support programs are last-ditch efforts to save what has been lost for a long time. The future lies with Archer Daniels Midland and not with the farm of forty or eighty or 160 acres.

The plight of the Webster family is a microcosm for American agriculture. When the mules are worn out and either die or have to be sold, when the flooding river wipes out the first planting, when the bank refuses further loans, small farmers never have enough money to ride out the bad weather. Bully tells Cleveland after the floods have washed out the cotton crop, "We made our cotton crop for the river again," and the narrator tells us that "the bank had carried him [Bully] about as far as it was going to. It was too much to expect the bank to let him have more money when his crop was gone and there would be no way for him to make a payment in the fall."

Ground down by fate and nature and bad luck, Bully, like

so many others in the American twentieth century, has to give up the independence of farm life, and, like those unfortunates who left the Edenic glow of Goldsmith's "Deserted Village" to forage for themselves in the cities, uproots his family and moves into Navasota to work in the oil mill. In all likelihood Daly will become somebody's maid, and the children will drift into the ranks of the unemployed. World War II saved many from the poverty of the tenant farms and small towns, but it is not likely that soldiering will save Hoodoo and Vincent and Tina and Little Suster from the lowest rungs of the underclass.

The focus character of the novel is Bully's son Cleveland, a man tormented by jealousy, filled with impotent rage against "Mr. John," often angry at the other sharecroppers, and mean enough to kick Joe Coby's white dog at the beginning of the novel. Cleveland is the hope of the Webster family, but the cards are so stacked against him – and his anger so frustrates him – that life threatens to overwhelm him for most of the novel. But Ruby Lee's patience and love finally make him see what a good and faithful wife she is. This helps to free him from the anger that has racked him for so long. In the final scene, when Cleveland is walking back to his father-in-law's house where he and Ruby Lee will live until the baby is born, he even makes peace with Joe Coby's white dog. It is with this reconciliation between dog and man that we see the real character of Cleveland finally blossom. He is a good man, and he will endure – perhaps prevail – after all.

A final word about the title. *High John the Conqueror* obviously refers to John Chaney, the rich plantation owner who holds sway over the poor sharecroppers and day laborers of the cotton lands. He is high in rank and conquers land and peoples. But there is also a play on High John the Conqueror root, which has a life in the world of superstition. Having some of the root in your pocket protected you from your enemies by giving you power. Herb shops all across the South sold High John root, and many people along the Navasot carried the root in their pockets the way some carry a rabbit's foot or a buckeye. High John can still be bought in Voodoo shops (often under the name Juan el Conquistador) as a brown liquid potion sold in quarter-ounce bottles. Sprinkle a few drops here and there and you can gain power over others. Recently, High John root has made an appearance as a hot new remedy for depression. In its newest incarnation, it is called St. John's Wort and comes in capsules that sell for about ten cents each. In the sophisticated world of herbal remedies, High John the Conqueror root does not promise power over others, but in the unsophisticated world of voodoo shops, Juan el Conquistador is still as potent in its way as John Chaney was in John W. Wilson's fine novel about life along the Brazos and Navasot bottoms.

James Ward Lee